HE'S A KID

A wise-cracking, tough-talking lonely kid. And she's a rich housewife from the glittering suburbs of L.A.

JUST A KID

Everything inside her shouted over and over. Just a kid. Just one year older than her son. Nineteen. A parking lot attendant, for Christ's sake . . .

AND YET

Something happened every time she was with him. Indescribable, the *energy* between them. Honest, simple . . . natural . . . somehow. No matter where he came from. No matter what his age. Together they could fill the emptiness, taking it as it came . . . living . . . loving . . .

MOMENT BY MOMENT

LILY TOMLIN *   JOHN TRAVOLTA *

MOMENT BY MOMENT

Written and Directed by
JANE WAGNER

Produced by
ROBERT STIGWOOD

Executive Producer
KEVIN McCORMICK

Associate Producers . . . . Bob LeMond and
                              Lois Zetter
Production Designers . . . . . Harry Horner
Director of Photography . . Philip Lathrop, A.S.C.
Film Editor . . . . John F. Burnett

A Robert Stigwood Production

A Universal Pictures Release

Panavision ®

Technicolor ®

MOMENT BY MOMENT

Darcy O'Brien

Based on the screenplay written by
Jane Wagner

A David Obst Book

BALLANTINE BOOKS • NEW YORK

MOMENT BY
MOMENT

One

IT was one of those Malibu parties. Strip Harrison, valet parking attendant, was hoping to clear twenty-five or thirty dollars before the night was over. After almost two years' picking up extra change this way, Strip was used to these parties. The behavior of the guests, who could be anything from friendly to rude, generous to stingy, rarely fazed him now.

Strip sat on the running board of an antique Rolls, nursing a joint to take the edge off things. The money was not bad but he was getting tired of playing the servant. Guests rarely talked to him except to call for their cars or ask him to run for cigarettes, and on a summer night like this, with the pure sea air, the music, and the muffled sound of conversation, he was apt to feel left out. Not that he felt he belonged inside, not yet. He was nineteen, a good-looking, dark-haired kid who had left home five years before to make it in Los Angeles. He was still at loose ends but had managed to stay out of trouble, and now he was beginning to realize that he had to focus on something, if someday he was going to find himself inside one of these parties and not parking cars the rest of his life.

He exhaled his joint and relaxed. It was the middle of the party, about ten o'clock, when nothing usually happened unless somebody got too drunk too soon. And from what he could tell, this was more of a white-wine crowd, joggers and tennis players who cared more about being sharp in the morning than letting themselves go at night. That was how they got rich and stayed rich, Strip figured.

They had behaved pretty decently to him so far. Even when there was condescension in their tone, Strip appreciated it when people bothered to be polite to him and tried to make some sort of conversation. A beautiful night, some would say, so clear, not like last night. You couldn't do much with that, but it was better than the ones who looked right through him, as though he didn't exist or were too insignificant to see. A remark about the Rams or the Dodgers could lead to some friendly banter that broke the tedium of getting in and out of cars all night long. There had been one jerk this night who had treated Strip to an asinine lecture about not scratching his Mercedes, but Strip had kept his cool, given out a few yessirs and nosirs, and nothing had come of it except the temptation to run the Mercedes into a telephone pole. Three years ago he would have been inclined to come back with a few smart remarks. But he had learned the hard way that it was easier to stay cool. Basically, Strip's instinct was to like people and to trust them, no matter who they were. He had been burned a few times, but it was not in his nature to be suspicious or hostile.

Strip amused himself by observing people closely. He did not care for the appearance of many of the men. They looked tan, lean and healthy, most of them, but, he thought to himself, they seemed to want to look like pimps, with their medallions and bracelets and flashy open shirts. Still, Strip wondered, what would he dress like if he had the money? Probably the same. It was the style around here. He thought of his own pitiful wardrobe. Tonight he was wearing olive-green army pants and a white T-shirt, not from any sense of style, simply from lack of money. His few good things he saved for going to Hollywood discos.

But if Strip had reservations about the men, he had few about the women. Many of them were spectacular, and one of his little games was making eye contact with them. The natural look of a couple of years before had given way to frantic hair styles, frizzy and wild, and make-up that was at war with reality. Strip thought the effect was terrific: It made the women look alive and exotic. He didn't mind the sheer cotton blouses either. Often, as he slipped behind the wheel of a newly arrived car, the woman's perfume would linger. His job had its little pleasures.

The party was being given by people named Rawlings, and they had one of the largest, most elegant beach houses Strip had ever seen. It sat right on the beach, on a private road called Latigo Shores Drive, and Strip could not even guess what the house was worth. Five hundred and fifty thousand at least, he thought. Megabucks. Idling about, Strip heard Bee Gees' sounds drifting through the air and, typically his curious self, he poked through some shrubbery and found a window to peek in. He saw people standing around in groups chatting and holding, sure enough, mostly wine glasses. It was a crowd of mixed ages, late twenties to late forties, and they seemed to be enjoying themselves, a little restrained perhaps, but having fun. Here and there couples danced the latest disco steps.

A woman with dark, straight hair and pale skin caught his eye. She was dancing, but not with much exuberance, and talking to her partner, a big, heavyset guy with a serious, maybe even slightly angry expression. She looked to be somewhere in her thirties, he over forty. Strip did not remember parking their car, and he wondered whether they were the Rawlings'. They were talking a lot and their dancing slowed, getting out of sync with the music. Strip was drawn to the woman's appearance, though she was dressed more soberly than most of her guests in a plain blouse and pants, and her hair hung simply, unpermed. Suddenly she broke from her partner, though the music had not stopped. She moved alone, over toward the window, looking grave, and Strip stepped aside so he would not be taken for a peeping Tom. He could still see her. He watched one hand go to her head and thought he saw her shudder or tremble. Other guests watched her surreptitiously but did not approach her, as though they sensed something they did not wish to get involved in. She slumped and leaned against a chair. Her dancing partner had disappeared into a crowd at the other end of the room. For what seemed like minutes, the woman stayed there, head in hand. Strip thought that if he had been a guest inside, he would have gone over to her to see what was the matter.

Then the woman drew herself up and strode quickly out of sight, toward the front door. Strip heard it open and slam, and he hurried over, thinking the woman must be ill. When he got there, she was leaning against a corner of the garage, both hands to her face, breathing deeply, and Strip could not tell whether she was near tears or about to be sick. He rushed up to her, then hesitated, not wanting to embarrass her. Finally he asked her if there was anything he could do.

"No, thank you. Yes. You could get me my car."

Up close Strip could see that it was her emotions and not her stomach bothering her.

"Are you all right?" he asked. Somebody had done something to her. "Which car is yours?"

"It's in there," she said, gesturing at the garage. "I'm Trisha Rawlings. You'll have to move those others."

Three other cars were blocking the garage door and Strip set about moving them. So that's Mrs. Rawlings, he thought. Her party, and something's gone wrong. Strip had never so much as talked to Trisha Rawlings or to her husband, Stuart. A secretary had hired him. As he moved the cars he looked at her and sensed her fragility. Yet there was strength in her too. Whatever had happened, she was determined to get away from it and act on her own. He wanted to wish her good luck.

There were as many Mercedeses as bathrooms in this part of town, but hers was a classic 1966 sedan. Strip was glad Mrs. Rawlings had something different. I want to like her, he thought. She's lonely outside her house with her own party going on.

"Can I do anything else for you?" he asked, holding the door for her.

"You're very nice," she said. "Yes, there is something else. Would you mind going inside and getting my dog? I want to take her with me." When Strip hesitated, she assured him it was only a little Maltese and had never bitten anyone.

"It's not that," Strip said. "I ain't afraid of dogs. It's the way I'm dressed." Having said it, he felt silly.

"No one will care," she said.

"Course not," he said. "Be right back. I guess I'll know which it is. Can't be very many dogs in there."

"Judge for yourself," she said, and they shared a laugh.

Inside, Strip zeroed in on his prey, hardly looking around at the house and the people. He was self-conscious and aware of the richness of the furnishings and the guests, but the dog came up to greet him almost immediately and he was in and out of the house in less than a minute.

"Come on, Scamp, we're going for a ride," Trisha said, hugging the dog to her. "That's a good girl."

"Scamp's a funny name for a girl dog," Strip said.

"That's what she is," Trisha said. "She's a little scamp, aren't you, Scamp?"

"I hope everything's all right," Strip said.

"It isn't," she said. "Maybe it will be. Listen, I really appreciate your being so kind. Here, let me give you something."

"Not a chance. It's not every night I get a chance to, you know. Parking cars can get pretty boring."

"I can imagine. What's your name?"

"Strip. Like in Sunset. Strip Harrison."

"Well, good night, Strip. Thanks."

She got into the car and Strip watched her drive toward the city, watched until the lights of her car blinked out.

Two

TWO days later Strip walked into Schwab's Drugstore on Bedford Drive in Beverly Hills and spotted Trisha Rawlings at the prescription counter. He had an urge to go up and say hello, but he held back. She was dressed in a silk shirt and skirt and as she stood there, waiting for a prescription to be filled, Strip could sense her nervousness. It was the first time he had seen her in bright light and he could not tell her age, except that she had to be well out of her twenties.

The pharmacist caught his eye and Strip moved to the counter without greeting Trisha.

"May I help you?"

"I'm looking for Greg McAlister," Strip said. "Your delivery boy. Didn't he show up for work, or what?"

The pharmacist, a young man doing his best to look older, gave Strip a severe look. "I doubt if it'll come as a surprise to you. We caught your friend, if that's what he is, with his hand in the cookie jar. Now if you don't mind, I've got customers. Who is next, please?"

There were no other customers, only Trisha, waiting and trying not to notice Strip, who had paled and felt his knees go weak at the ugly news.

"Wow," Strip said, trying to show astonishment at something he had long been afraid was going to happen. "So that's what. I am, you know, I am really . . . dumbfounded!" He imagined the scene. Greggie grabbed, handcuffed, dragged away. Where were they holding him?

"Oh, yes," said the pharmacist, "I'm sure it's all a big surprise to you. Mrs. Rawlings, here is your prescription. Thank you very much."

"What about the Seconal?" Trisha asked. "I'll be at the beach for a while." The pharmacist peered over his glasses. "I wanted a supply, you see. I can't keep coming into town."

"I'm sorry, Mrs. Rawlings. They're clamping down. You've probably read about it. You'll have to get your doctor to renew this."

"Where can I find him?" Strip said. "Where did they take him?"

"It's out of my hands," the pharmacist said, watching Trisha clasp her bag sharply shut in frustration. She turned to walk out. "Have a pleasant weekend, Mrs. Rawlings," he called after her. "I envy you at the beach." She left without replying.

"Look," Strip said, trying to keep his composure against his rising anger at the pharmacist's indifference, "what do you mean it's out of your hands? You're a human being, aren't you? Where did they take him? Where are they holding him?"

"I mean it's in the hands of the law. If you want to help your friend, I suggest you call a lawyer. That's all the free advice I can give."

"Lawyers cost money," Strip said.

"I wouldn't dispute you there. Probably it'll take more money than you've ever seen to get your friend out."

Strip would have taken anyone's advice at that moment. He was so anxious about his friend that he had no strength to challenge the pharmacist's callousness.

Outside. the sunshine hit him like a search-light. He hesitated, not sure what to do next, feeling weak and sick to his stomach. He propped himself against the side of the build-ing and tried to think straight. Greggie was in serious trouble now, and Strip felt conflicting emotions toward him. Mostly he was afraid for him and confused about how to help him, but Strip also felt angry at him for being stupid. Getting caught had been inevitable, and Strip had tried to convince Greggie of this for months. Now Strip was involved too, and he resented it. He would do anything for his friend and he did not love him any the less, but why hadn't Greggie listened? There had been no arguing with him. Every time Strip had got after him, Greggie would say something like "I don't wanna spend my life parking cars. I'm gonna score early." You couldn't deal with that.

There was a phone booth on the corner. Strip thumbed through the Yellow Pages look-ing under lawyers, sensing that this was a stupid way to go about it. He ought to know someone to contact, but he didn't. He had just figured out that lawyers prefer to call them-selves attorneys when he caught sight of Trisha Rawlings on the other side of the street. Instinctively he hurried across, oblivious to the traffic, and followed her into a shop called The Cookstore, glancing at himself in the windows and smoothing back his hair as he went in.

The shop was small and dark, with rich-smelling coffee beans displayed in open barrels, tin scoops plunged into them. One wall was lined with teas in gaily colored boxes. Positioning himself next to the cash register, Strip tried to take up an appealing pose, a thumb hooked into his belt, concealing his anxiety with a show of nonchalance. He watched Trisha examine an espresso pot.

"You ought to get one of those," the storekeeper was saying.

"I can never get them to work properly," Trisha said. "They're always spraying boiling water at me."

Strip watched her hands fidgeting. He wondered what was wrong with her, why she needed Seconal, whether she was still bothered by whatever had happened at the party. He assumed she had had some sort of fight with her husband, but could it still be going on? He was disturbed to find her in this state. There was something about her, an appealing unaffectedness, that made him sense that she was a decent, kind woman, and Strip told himself that, whatever was wrong in her life, she didn't deserve it.

The storekeeper scooped up dark beans and let them slide into a coffee grinder. Then he added a scoop of lighter beans and started the machine.

"You're sure that's the blend I like?"

"I got a better memory for what my customers like than they have. You like French roast mostly with a third Guatemalan."

He bagged the finely ground coffee and moved to the cash register. Trisha followed and found herself next to Strip, who looked into her face, smiling.

"Hello again," he said, very friendly. "We met before, you know? Remember me? Sure you do."

"Yes," Trisha said, not really looking at him. "How are you?" She had the air of someone who did not wish to be rude but who would clearly prefer to remain alone and unrecognized. "How much is that?" she asked the storekeeper, digging into her handbag.

"Five sixty-five, Mrs. Rawlings."

"You feel better?" Strip asked.

"Just fine, thank you. If you'll excuse me, I have a lot of errands to run."

From the doorway, Strip called good-bye to her as she left the shop. She had seemed embarrassed at seeing and talking to him, but he was not insulted. People didn't like to be caught with their defenses down, and he had been with her at a vulnerable moment. Still, he wanted to talk to her, for exactly what reason, he wasn't sure. She had seemed grateful to him the other night. She might be able to advise him now. She looked sensible.

"You want coffee, young man?" the storekeeper asked.

"Huh? Hey, no, no. I, uh, I drink tea."

"I got all kinds, China, Ceylon, India, Taiwan." The man made a sweeping gesture toward the wall of tea as though summoning the mysteries of the East. But he was a dumpy little fellow and didn't look the part of the magician.

"Look, I use instant, okay?" said Strip, and he hurried out.

He spotted Trisha in a crowd up the block and ran after her. Before she could protest, he had taken her packages from her and started up a new line of chat:

"Listen, I'll help with these bags and let me explain to you. I don't mean to bug you. I just wanted to say hello and see how you were, because I was a little worried about you that night. Everything work out okay?"

"I'm fine," Trisha said.

"I'm really glad." He knew that everything was not fine with her, but he did not want to be too direct. "The funny thing is," he went on, "I got my own problems today."

"You do?" she said, looking at him for the first time.

He had been expecting her to ask if there was anything she could do to help, but when she did not, he plunged ahead. He told her that his best friend, the fellow he had been living with, had been arrested. He said that he had just heard the news from the pharmacist, the same one who had refused to fill her prescription. Strip hoped that this touch would make her feel some camaraderie with him since they had both received bad news from the same source, but while she did not seem wholly indifferent, she kept on walking without responding. Her manner, while neither really cold nor aloof, was that of someone reluctant to get involved in someone else's problems. Probably because, Strip guessed compassionately, she had enough of her own. He was grateful to her for listening to him at all. At least he had found someone to talk to.

"I guess the only thing to do is call a lawyer," he said. "I was gonna call a lawyer. I don't know about my lawyer. I think he's out of town. I was lookin' in the phone book. Jesus, there must be a hundred thousand lawyers in this town."

"Lawyers and doctors," Trisha said.

"Yeah."

They were heading for a parking lot on the corner and before Strip knew it she was getting into the old Mercedes and closing the door. Her mind must really be somewhere else, he thought. He was holding her packages and she seemed to be ready to drive off without them.

"You forgot these," Strip said.

"Oh," Trisha said. "Thank you." She took them through the window. "I don't know what I was thinking of."

"You look kinda wired," Strip said. She ignored this.

"Imagine if I'd left them with you," Trisha said.

"I'd of brought them to you."

"You would? That's very nice. But you don't know—oh, of course you do. You did the parking. I'm sorry. Here. You've been very kind. Again. Let me give you something."

"That's the second time. I told you before, my pleasure."

Strip looked into her face, which still betrayed nervousness and confusion. It was a nice face, pale, framed by her dark hair. It looked like a face that would have a hard time being phony. He did not want to see her drive off.

"I tell you what you could do, you could give me a lift," he said. Maybe if he had some time with her, she could help him about Greggie. And besides, it would be nice to take a little drive with her. "I know just how you felt that night," he said. "You were really lost, weren't you? I feel a little that way now, on account of what's happened with my friend."

"Which way are your going?"

"If you could take me anywhere near like Sunset and Western, that'd be great."

Trisha was silent for a moment, staring straight ahead. She seemed to be pondering the wisdom of giving him a ride. Strip knew she was going in the opposite direction, but there was no point in pretending he was going somewhere he was not. He hoped she would decide to take him. Why shouldn't she? He wasn't exactly coming on like a rapist.

"I'm sorry," she said finally. "I'm heading in the opposite direction."

"I know," he said. He let that sink in but she said nothing more, looking only like a person who was beginning to be very anxious to get away. Strip was disappointed but he found himself unable to resent her. "It was nice seeing you again," he said. "Hope you cheer up." Then he turned slowly and walked away.

Three

STRIP'S last remark hit Trisha pretty hard. She had not wanted to be so transparent. Her style was to keep her problems to herself, especially when she felt on edge emotionally, as she did now. That boy had seen her close to breaking down on the night of the party. Evidently he had seen enough to be able to read her mood today. In a way she felt stupid about not giving him a lift, although she usually did not go around giving lifts to near strangers. His manner was sweet and understanding, and he had some big problem of his own, something she had not fully taken in because of her distractions. She was getting sick of being unable to think straight. That was why she was going to the beach house, alone, to get herself calmed down and straightened out. The Seconal would have helped, but she would do without it.

She would stop at the Bel-Air house, pick up some things, and head for the beach. As she reached Sunset and swung west, images of Strip floated through her mind. She imagined driving in the car with him, listening to his problems. Maybe that would have been good for her, taking on someone else's burden, if only for a few minutes. She thought about him and realized that she found him attractive. This made her laugh. That was all she needed, a flirtation with someone young enough to be her son. What was she thinking? What made her think she was attractive to him at all? He felt sorry for her, that was all. Trisha did not enjoy people feeling sorry for her, and she thought, What a rotten basis to get to know someone. Pity. Still, that could not be the whole of it. He had wanted something from her: advice, help. Why did he turn to her? He hardly knew her. He must be desperate. Or was he just throwing her a line?

It seemed that lately she could not make up her mind about anything or anyone. Was her life coming apart? Stu was running around with someone else. Not the most earthshaking thing in the world, except that Stu's affair was the sign and culmination of something worse, that they had ceased being a part of one another. How had it happened? Whatever it was that had held them together for eighteen years —romance, their son Tim, habit, routine, memories, property, friends in common, a whole life in common—it all seemed to have grown dim and insubstantial. Love. Did she still love Stu? She thought she did. Surely the prospect of living without him was unnerving. She was not one to cry often, but now she felt frequently on the verge of tears. She would catch herself watching the corniest television program or movie and it would hit her like the world's most profound tragedy.

Lately her head had been filled with detached images—a dinner party or a vacation or a talk she had enjoyed with Stu or Tim. These things would shift before her with no apparent reason or connection to one another. And with Stu, everything seemed to be taking place in a vacuum. Their last trip together: It had been to France, the previous summer, and she might as well have gone alone. No fighting, nothing as tangible as that, nothing to make her angry or desperate: Only a kind of blurry nothingness, conversations about nothing, silences, lovemaking that had all the zest of a dinner of cold cuts. And now Stu was carrying on with this girl. It was as though he were trying to smash everything. Trisha left open the possibility that he did not know what he was doing. She could understand why he would be attracted to someone like Stacy. But how could she tell him that she understood? Understood in spite of her jealousy. For that he would at least have to ask her how she felt, and he had not. She would go to the beach house, alone, for an indefinite period, start sleeping the night through again, steady herself.

She drove through the gates of Bel-Air and along Bellagio Drive to her own gates, which were set in a high white wall, the entrance to a preserve within a preserve. She pressed the electric-eye device in her car to open the gates and started up the driveway, switching off the tape cassette, opening the window to let in the quiet and the fresh air.

It was a large, elegant house in the Spanish style, built in the 1930s by a movie director who had wanted to live like a Prince de Bourbon on a slightly reduced scale. The Rawlingses had bought it seven years earlier. Trisha would have been content with something less grand but it was a sign, after all, of the enormous success of Stu's real-estate business, and they could well afford it. A gardener came three times a week, and he was there now, as Trisha parked and got out. Only the rhythmic whish-whish of the sprinklers and the sharp snap of the gardener's shears, as he perfected an already symmetrical hedge, broke the silence. There had been times—years—when Trisha had found the silence and peace of this place soothing. Now she found them oppressive. She wanted to gather up her things and head for the beach as quickly as possible.

The pool repairman was bearing down on her from around a corner of the house. She did not want to deal with him now. Something about a filter. She waved him off with as much courtesy as she could muster.

Maria, the maid, greeted her at the door, and Scamp performed her ritual, bringing a ball, dropping it, and fetching it gleefully when Trisha threw it.

"Do you need help with anything from the car, Mrs. Rawlings?"

"No, Maria, thank you. It's all going to the beach."

Trisha went up to her bedroom immediately. She felt something of a stranger in the house today. Even her bedroom, so large and airy, the light diffused by the huge trees stirring outside the windows, seemed less inviting than usual. She loved that room. Its light blues and greens suited her, and she could lie on the chaise reading for hours, Scamp always curled at her feet.

She put a few last things into a suitcase already almost packed. She wouldn't need much.

"I know she's on her way to the beach. I just want to talk to her a second before she leaves."

Naomi's voice. Trisha could hear her coming up the stairs. Naomi was her closest friend, and Trisha loved her, but she was not anxious to see her now. An image of Strip, standing by her car, flashed into Trisha's mind, and she felt a wave of affection for the boy. It was a small enough thing, but that someone had paid attention to her and had wanted something from her meant something today. No, she would not tell Naomi about him. Naomi would only think she was trying to buck herself up with the notion that a teenager had tried to make time with her.

Naomi came into the room tentatively.

"How do you feel? Are you holding up?"

"Sure." Seeing Naomi made Trisha feel better. Naomi would be her friend no matter what. She was glad now that Naomi had dropped by. They had known each other for nearly fifteen years. Naomi was a striking, chic blonde, in conventional terms sexier and more beautiful than Trisha. Yet both understood that Trisha was the more independently minded of the two, the more accepting of wild or erratic behavior among their other friends, and the more inclined to go her own way regardless of trend or fashion. They made a good pair. Trisha could get from Naomi the latest news or gossip, and Naomi could get from Trisha a judgment unaffected by anything except what Trisha thought was true or fair.

"You're going to the beach," Naomi said in

her low, well-modulated voice. "Any special reason? I mean, you just got back, darling."

"You know why, Naomi. Stu and I haven't been getting along at all."

"Sweetheart, I know the party was a disaster for you, but really, a little spat is hardly reason to pack your bags."

Trisha told Naomi that she was not walking out. She simply needed to be alone for a few days. She and Stu couldn't seem to be in the same room together without getting on each other's nerves.

Naomi knew the Rawlingses as a happy and compatible couple. They spent a lot of money on their houses and vacations, but they were conservative about marriage and worked to keep their lives together. It was true that as Stu's business prospered, he had become more and more involved in it, and occasionally Trisha had complained that she did not see enough of him. But it was hard for Naomi to imagine what could be seriously wrong now. Trisha looked overwrought, under strain. Her pale skin, always becoming, now looked like pallor.

"What is it, Trisha?" Naomi came over and put her hands gently on her friend's shoulders. "Tell me. Maybe I can help."

Trisha had not wanted to talk about it, but Naomi's tone and touch loosened her. She felt her throat tighten and she murmured:

"Stu's having an affair with Stacy. The young assistant he hired."

"How do you know that?"

"I'm not dumb, and I'm a realist. He's been acting strange for several weeks. Then at the party—" Her voice broke. When she managed to get control, she said, "At the party. I was dancing with him. I wasn't enjoying it. It was like, I don't know, he wasn't there, or I wasn't. Then I realized he was watching Stacy the whole time he was dancing with me. I said something to him about it. I was trying not to be bitchy. Just letting him know I was there, that I was concerned. He got very defensive and nasty. Called me a damn fool. He apologized right away, but I felt sure he would rather be with Stacy and it was too much for me. I had to get out. I couldn't face anybody."

Trisha sank into a chair and put her head in her hands. Naomi came over and sat down on the rug next to her.

"I think this whole thing is ridiculous," Naomi said. "If Stu's fallen for that child, he's lost his sanity. I'm sure he'll regain it quickly. I'm not sure I believe any of it anyway."

"There's nothing ridiculous about it. Stacy works with him every day. She's very attractive and she's involved in the business. That's a pretty strong combination where Stu's concerned."

"Nonsense," Naomi said. "She's obviously nothing but a ruthless career girl trying to get to the top in the oldest way in the world. I have too much respect for Stu to imagine he'd be taken in by that."

"I'm afraid there's more to it," Trish said. "I wouldn't be surprised if she were in love with him."

"Even so, which I don't for a minute believe. She's nothing compared to you."

31

This provoked a small, unfelt laugh from Trisha, who knew that Naomi was trying to joke her out of her anxiety. But there did not seem to be much that was funny about the situation. Trisha felt powerless. She knew that all she had now was herself. She felt she had to concentrate on not losing that.

"I feel like some goddamned *Ms.* magazine character," Trisha said. "Eighteen years of marriage and then, bang, suddenly you realize it was a mistake to get married in college. What am I? A housewife. Mother. When all of a sudden I'm not either one anymore. Tim's away for good, or almost. What am I supposed to do? I thought I was enjoying life. What a joke."

"Come on," Naomi said. "You're acting like it's the end of the world, and it isn't even the end of your marriage. If you knew what confidence I have in you and Stu, together. Listen, you're an example to us all. You can't fall apart at the first sign of strain."

"I'm not falling apart."

"Of course you're not."

Trisha got up and put a sweater into her bag, saying she wanted to get down to the beach. This house was depressing her, and Stu might come home. She didn't want a confrontation.

"Promise me one thing," Naomi said. "You won't rush into a divorce. That would be idiotic. You can tell me to mind my own business, but I know Stu and I know Stacy well enough. Even if what you think is true, it's not going to last at all. Believe me." Trisha said nothing, and Naomi added: "Divorce is not the answer any more than marriage is."

"What's that supposed to mean?" Trisha said.

"It means that life is complicated. Sometimes you just have to live with the complications. For a while. Then things straighten themselves out." She went over to Trisha. "There's a lot to be said, an awful lot to be said for the status quo. At least it's familiar."

"You're probably right," Trisha said.

"And you know that underneath this five-hundred-dollar muumuu, there's a shoulder to cry on."

"I know that, Naomi," Trisha said, holding out her arms, and the two women embraced.

"Call you tomorrow or the next day," Naomi said. "I have a leg wax at Arden's and I'll fill you in on all the gossip."

"This month," said Trisha, "it's liable to be about me."

Four

___

UNDER a half moon Trisha played with Scamp on the beach, the air cool, strong salt smells off the sea. She chased the little dog along the white edge of the surf and threw the ball again and again. She splashed Scamp, raced her, ran zig-zag up and down the beach.

From shadows between houses Strip watched, pleased to see her free and playful, entranced by her long, angular body, graceful in the starlight and moonlight. Tiny, dancing drops of moonlight reflected off her caftan as she whirled this way and that, sending up spurts of sand. Finally she collapsed onto a blanket. She put her arms under her head and picked out the stars, as Scamp nuzzled her, coaxing her to one more throw. Music from a radio grew louder and softer as the waves retreated, rose again, crashed.

He had just arrived in Malibu. He wore a backpack, which he unslung and dropped onto the sand, pulling from it a small envelope. He took off his shoes, left the pack on the ground, and started toward Trisha, calling out, "Hey there! I got something for ya!"

Scamp barked dutifully and ran to greet him, and Trisha watched as Strip let the dog jump up on him and lifted her into his arms.

"You came all the way out here to give me a present?"

"Hell, no," Strip said, drawing back and acting somewhat offended. "I got friends." He looked at her as though he were asking for a retort. "The thing is," he rushed on, "they invited me out for the weekend and I figured if maybe I bumped into you on the beach, I could give you some reds." He held out the envelope again. "Here."

She took it and looked at it.

"They're one hundred percent pharmaceutical. Trust me."

Trisha was amused, and asked where they'd come from. Strip said nothing but grinned and gave her a conspiratorial look.

"Guess," he said. "Think."

"Schwab's!" Trisha laughed.

"Hey! I made you smile."

"And these will make me sleep?"

"Sure. I hate to think of you tossin' and turnin' all night."

Funny he would say that, Trisha thought. Already she had concluded that tonight would be the first time in weeks that she would be able to sleep through without pills. The sound of the sea would be enough. She looked inside the envelope.

"You didn't give me very many. Cheapskate!"

"Uh, well." Strip looked at a wave breaking in the moonlight. "Pretty, huh? The thing is, I didn't actually know if you wanted 'em for the right reasons. These days, everywhere you look, people o.d.'ing all over the place. You looked like you had some split nerve ends."

"Come on," Trisha said. "You're holding out the rest to sell, I bet. I'll pay for these."

"Hey, no. I don't want you to. I don't like to encourage pill poppin'."

Trisha picked up her radio, blanket, and Scamp's ball and started toward the house.

"You goin'? Wait." Strip followed her.

"Look," Trisha said, quickening her pace, "I'm not addicted to pills, if that's what you think." She stopped and stared at him. "Is that what you think?"

"No." Strip's shoulders sank. He was a child caught in a fib. "I'll be honest with you, okay? You had me down right. I was, it's true. I was gonna sell the rest."

"No wonder you and your friends need lawyers. Is that what you do for a living? Whatever happened to valet parking?"

She had reached the steps to her house. Strip hurried along behind her.

"Hey, Miss Ultra-frost! You gonna turn me in? Gonna call in the narcs?" He stood with his hands on his hips, mimicking her hauteur. "You know what? I think you think you're better than me. You think you're superior to me? Boy, that's really great. You're fallin' apart or loaded or whatever it was you were the other night, and you're real friendly. When you want somethin'. I can see it was dumb as hell of me to try and do you a favor."

She was halfway up the steps to the deck. She paused, somewhat chastened, thinking she must have sounded awfully uptight and censorious. "I'm sorry," she said. "Thank you for bringing me the pills. It was very thoughtful of you."

Strip came up a couple of steps after her.

"Hey," he said. "Am I chasin' you away? Want to go swimmin'?"

"No, thanks."

"It's warm enough."

"I know. I'm tired."

"Maybe you won't need no pills."

"Maybe."

They looked at each other in silence for what seemed a minute.

"I love that thing you got on," Strip said finally. "It shines like it's got mirrors."

He reached up and took hold of her sleeve. Trisha moved back but he held fast, his thumb moving quickly over the material.

"Damn if it doesn't have mirrors," he said. "A million little mirrors. Beautiful." He looked into her face.

"Please let go," Trisha said. He released her, and she started up the steps again.

"Here," Strip said. "Let me help with the radio."

"It weighs about two pounds," Trisha said. She continued on up the steps to the sun deck. "Come on, Scamp."

Strip stood looking up at her. "You know, if you'd go swimming, you wouldn't need pills to make you sleep."

"I might not need them anyway."

"Hey, wait. Listen, can you hear me? I'll come up."

"I can hear you," Trisha said over the roar of a wave. "What is it?"

Someone passing by might have thought that they were rehearsing a scene from *Romeo and Juliet*. Strip was halfway up the steps, craning up at Trisha, who leaned down toward him over the railing of the sun deck. I should toss him a rose, she was thinking. She found his persistence rather appealing.

"We should keep in touch," Strip said. He was scrambling for dialogue now. "As long as I'm around, see, you won't have to worry about sleeping. You won't ever have to suffer the humiliation of tryin' to get pills legal. What I mean is, like I was really embarrassed for you at Schwab's. Who needs that, right? What a phony that guy was. I swear, I felt like bustin' him one. Right in the mouth."

She moved toward the screen door of the house as Strip tried to slow her with a waterfall of words. He told her that he couldn't stand to think of her tossing and turning at night. It wasn't right. She needed her beauty sleep. She should take care of herself. The very thought of her lying there awake at night upset him tremendously.

"Good-bye," Trisha said mildly.

"Wait." He was on the top step now. "Hey, listen. Can I tell you something sincerely? From my heart?"

"No." She opened the screen door and went inside. Strip followed and now they faced each other through the screen.

"It's important," Strip said. "Because I just lied to you."

"How shocking," she said, amused. "I can't believe it. A fine, upstanding fellow like yourself?"

"I want to level with you because I don't like to lie to people I like. I make it a policy. I mean

41

—there are enough people I don't like so I have enough people I can lie to."

"Look," she said, getting just a trifle exasperated with him, "those four little pills don't mean I've relinquished my right to privacy. I'm beginning to think it's easier dealing with Schwab's."

Strip held out his arms, looking every inch the condemned man pleading for a commutation of sentence.

"Okay." Trisha gave in. "What?"

"When I said I hated to think of you tossin' and turnin' back there? Well, I was lyin'. The truth is," he said with a grin that was a little sheepish and a little devilish, "I like to think of it. In fact, I can't stop myself thinkin' of it."

This is getting rather too direct, Trisha said to herself. She had no comeback and suddenly felt self-conscious.

"It's just a confession," Strip said. "I thought I should come clean. Don't take it the wrong way. Okay?"

"You can bet I won't," she said. "Good night." She closed the door, gently.

Inside, Trisha leaned on the door and reflected with some amusement on the situation. She didn't mind being pursued, though it was true that she wanted to be alone. She could not quite figure Strip out. Given the way he lived, parking cars and selling pills and God knows what else, you wouldn't expect him to be so polite, almost gallant. He had come around to implying a sexual interest in her, but there was something so innocent about it. At thirty-six she was happy to encounter such innocence.

She switched on the light and thought about getting something to eat.

A knock. More knocks on the door.

"What now?" She sighed, just loud enough to be heard.

"Are you upset?" came his voice, punctuated by the sound of the ocean.

"I will be in a minute."

"Did you mean to leave Scamp out here? Because she's out here."

What had she been thinking, to leave Scamp out like that? She opened the door. Strip stood there with Scamp in his arms, looking pleased that he had found a way to make Trisha appear again.

"Yeah," he said, handing over the dog, "I kinda thought she was a house pet. A little dog like that. Say, that light's out."

"The fixture's broken."

"I'll fix it for you."

"No, no, thanks, I'm used to it. Oh, I think I hear the phone. Thanks again for the pills. Good night, Sam," she said firmly, closing the door.

Strip turned and hurried down to the beach. He had not heard any phone, and he was not pleased that she called him Sam.

Trisha set about resuming her independence. She flicked a switch and sent the runs of a Mozart piano concerto cascading through the house, which had speakers in every room. The ordered beauty of the music was perfection to her, and she thought with satisfaction of how she had left a wedge of brie to soften on the table in the breakfast room. She sat at the table eating the cheese and a quartered apple, gazing out at the movements of the sea, feeling something close to peace.

Then she spotted Strip. He was standing at the edge of the water, a silhouette. Does he want me to see him? Trisha wondered. He was testing the water with his foot. Then he pulled off his pants and tossed them backward onto dry sand. He waded into the water, slowly at first, then running, splashing and disappearing head first into a foamy, breaking wave. Trisha forced herself to turn away. She got up, put the cheese in the refrigerator and the dish in the sink, turned out the lights and went to bed.

Strip touched the smooth bottom with his feet. He could still stand. He turned back toward shore and saw the lights in Trisha's house go off one by one. He sensed a wave coming and moved out, let himself be lifted in its swell, and watched it roll and break. All the lights were out now. He swam farther out, using slow, strong strokes and kicking furiously until he reached a bed of kelp. The rubbery tentacles were unpleasant and frightening in the dark, and when he felt an endless piece brushing against his leg he arched himself and swam again, beyond the kelp, well beyond the wave line, where the water was black and well over his head. He thrashed about and swam until his body told him to quit, and then he moved back in and caught a wave, drawing his arms in under him for the brief, swift ride, washing up on the beach.

Trisha could not sleep. She moved about in her bed, feeling the unstirring lump of Scamp

at the foot, envying the dog's repose. She felt a
wave of compassion for Strip. She was beginning to sense that he was something of a lost
soul. She thought of his form plunging into the
sea and felt different emotions, stirrings. Then
she remembered numberless times when she
had watched Tim rush into the water like that,
and Stu, alone or with Tim, weekends of bliss-
ful beach laziness, and sadness invaded her.
Oh, God, she thought, don't let him destroy all
those years, all that happiness and peace. Don't
do it, Stu. And her sadness was mixed with
shame and a sense of betrayal and failure when
she thought of Stu with Stacy.

She told herself not to think like that. She
had to get to sleep, or tomorrow would be
wrecked. She wanted to get up early and have
breakfast on the deck. To feel healthy again.

She shook one of Strip's pills from the envelope and swallowed it. Then she reached
down for Scamp and hugged her.

Five

WHEN the ringing came to her through her heavy, drugged sleep, Trisha thought it was the alarm and that she was in Bel-Air lying in bed with Stu, and it occurred to her with sharp resentment that she did not want him to make love to her. Then she realized it was the phone and that she was at the beach, and she found herself hoping it was Stu.

It was. He apologized for waking her. Naomi had told him where she was. He had been worried.

"I was going to call," Trisha said. "Tell you I was out here." She sat up to clear her head.

"I thought we were going to see each other," Stu said. He reminded her that there was much to be decided. He kept on talking in a general way, getting no response. His matter-of-fact tone depressed Trisha. She was afraid she was going to cry, and she put her hand over the receiver so he couldn't hear her. "You seem so withdrawn," he said finally. "Like you're not there."

"I'm not," she managed to say in a clear voice. She visualized her husband. He would be sitting in his office or perhaps he was calling her from his Rolls. He enjoyed doing that. It was a part of his boyish quality, his love of toys.

"Don't leave this all up to me," Stu said. He sounded a bit plaintive. Trisha imagined a slightly pained look on his face. It was a handsome face, always tan from tennis and the beach, though it had gone jowly of late because he had been drinking too much. Trisha took some solace from knowing that this affair was rough on Stu's nerves.

"Did you hear me?" he said. "I said don't leave this all up to me."

"You left the marriage up to me," Trisha came back. "I'm leaving the divorce up to you. I hope you'll have better luck."

"Trish. Don't be unfair. You're . . . making this heavier than it has to be."

"Yes?"

"I miss you. I do."

"Wonderful. Am I supposed to jump for joy? You know, I really can't blame you for wanting Stacy. After all, she's so attractive and intelligent and devoted to her job. I mean, the girl really is dedicated, isn't she? You must have so many things to talk about. Mortgages and square footage. Buying and selling."

"Trish."

"Who's going to tell Tim?"

"Why tell him anything? There's no need, until he comes home again. I—then who knows?"

Trisha didn't know whether to encourage Stu's vacillations or not. Just now he was sounding like someone who didn't really know whether he wanted to be doing what he was doing. Did men behave like this just so they could be forgiven?

"I wish Tim would write," Trisha said. "Make sure Maria forwards my mail."

"You're going to be there for a while?"

"I may be. I have no idea."

"Look. Wait. What about . . . the pool filter?"

"What?"

"What do you want me to do about the pool filter?"

"Come on, Stu. I think you can handle that one yourself. Get Stacy's advice."

"I'll call you tomorrow. Or should I?"

"Call me any time you like. I am enjoying being alone, though, under the circumstances."

Trisha, fully awake now, hung up the phone and stretched luxuriously. Stu had sounded rather indecisive, and she didn't know whether this made her feel better or not. His confusions could have a way of adding to her own. She got up and fluffed her hair, looking at herself in the mirrors that covered one wall of the big, airy room, not displeased with what she saw. She was determined to enjoy the day. Through the window she saw that the fog was already burning off.

At about eleven, having had only the good coffee, she set about preparing lunch. Trisha was never one to let herself go to hell when alone. It was not her style to eat scraps or to let a dish sit unwashed. She liked to cook and was able to enjoy preparing a meal for the sensual and aesthetic pleasure of it, although now she did find herself wishing she had someone to share it with. She made chicken tarragon, which happened to be one of Stu's favorites.

By noon she was sitting on the beach with a book and the chicken and a chilled bottle of white wine. The book told the story of a Houston plastic surgeon who poisons his wife and is subsequently gunned down by his father-in-law. I could be worse off, Trisha thought, smiling to herself. The cold, dry wine tasted good with the food. She lifted the bottle from the sand and poured herself another glass, enjoying the slightly dizzying combination of alcohol and sun.

Surfers plied the small waves of Latigo Bay. Skillfully they maneuvered their boards, getting the most out of a lazy sea, blond Californians who would be back the next day and the next. Out of the corner of her eye Trisha noticed a lone body surfer, his foot raised up as a rudder, angling in on a wave some distance down the beach, where the row of houses gave way to a stretch of open sand. As he climbed to his feet, moving gingerly among rocks, she recognized Strip. Their eyes met and he waved and headed toward her. Scamp took off toward him, ball in teeth.

"Hope you got some sleep," Strip said, standing dripping before her in tank trunks and soaked T-shirt. "You don't mind me using your water, do you?"

"It belongs to the people," she said, making a politician's openhanded gesture. She was not unfriendly but not overly hospitable either. She had tried to establish a certain order and peace this morning and was reluctant to have it disturbed. Scamp had gotten herself soaked, and Trisha folded her in a towel and rubbed her.

"Hey, you got a towel to spare?" Strip asked.

"What happened to your friends? Don't they believe in towels at their place?"

"Guess what? They weren't even there. Some friends, huh? So I crashed on the beach. No blanket or nothin'. Some friends, huh?"

Trisha took a towel from her beach bag and tossed it to him, feeling a little guilty at her less-than-eager generosity. Obviously, he had no friends at the beach. Apparently his only friend was in jail. She poured herself more wine and nibbled at the chicken, watching Strip pull off his T-shirt and rub his chest. No fat on him at all, she noticed.

It was nearing one o'clock and Strip had eaten nothing since a doughnut and a cup of coffee the previous morning. Trisha put the chicken aside and Strip eyed it, trying to formulate some simple request for a reprieve from starvation.

"Why aren't you eatin' that chicken?" he asked. "Something the matter with it?"

"I'm finished."

"Yeah? You going to give it to Scamp or throw it away?"

Trisha handed him a piece, amused at his approach.

"Thanks. I hate waste." He tore into it. "Is that wine?" She passed him the bottle. He spread out his towel and sat down, taking a long swig of wine, feeling some sense of accomplishment.

"Yeah," he ruminated between bites. "All my friends are undependable, except for Greggie

53

and he's in jail. You like to cook? This is good."

"I'm fond of reading too," Trisha said. She tossed her book aside and rolled over, burying her head in her arms.

Undaunted, Strip turned for conversation to the design he noticed on his towel. It had a Princeton University seal on it.

"You go to Princeton?" he asked her.

"No. They didn't admit women when I was in school. My husband went and he wants my son to go, too."

"You got a son going to college? I never would of believed it."

"He is still in high school. I'm not that ancient."

"Didn't say you were. What's he gonna be, a lawyer?"

"He might eventually. He'll probably major in economics."

"Lawyers don't come cheap," Strip said. He was hoping she would pick up on this, but when she did not, he continued. "There are so many of 'em, but they seem to get plenty of business. The thing is, when you need a lawyer you can count on, it's rough, because how can you know? How do you know the guy won't take money from the other side?"

"There are still honest people in the world, believe it or not. You're much too cynical at your age."

"No, I'm not. I'm a nice guy. And just to prove it, whadda ya think, I've got some more pills for you."

Trish rolled over and faced him. She told

him forcefully that she did not need and did not want any more pills.

"And I think," she went on, "that it's a damned shame and a disgrace that a nice boy like you is risking ruining himself by getting involved with drugs and criminals."

"I was gonna tell you," Strip said, offended. "If you're into pills, I could get any kinda mood changer you want." There was sarcasm in his tone. "Ups, downs, tranks, amies, 'ludes."

"I am not *into* pills. You can't go on living this way, you know. It's going to catch up with you. It's already caught up with your friend!"

"Maybe you *should* be into pills. You need somethin' to mellow you out." He put the chicken back in the basket, pounded the cork back into the wine, and stood up. "I ain't hungry anymore, much as I hate waste. You know, it's great for people like you to be so goddamned moral. There's nothing like it, when you can afford it. And by the way, my name's not Sam. It's Strip. Like I told you. Just a little thing, a person's name."

He turned and trotted off down the beach, muttering loudly enough for her to hear, "A nice boy like me, huh? Wow. What a world!"

Trisha was upset. Now she didn't even feel like sunning herself. She well knew that Strip had been hinting that she should help him find a lawyer for his friend. She had not wanted to get involved in what she thought was a sordid business. She sensed something good in Strip. That was why she had made her little moral speech. But maybe he had a point too. And get-

ting his name wrong—that was embarrassing.
She noticed that he had left his T-shirt behind.
She looked down the beach for him, but he had
disappeared.

Fog billowed in early that afternoon and
made Trisha feel lonely. She telephoned Naomi
and told her she was enjoying her solitude, or
near-solitude.

"What's that?" said Naomi. "Visitors?"

"Not exactly. There's this kid hanging around.
He parked cars for us Saturday. He's rather
charming."

"Watch out for those types," Naomi said.
"They take you in with that indescribable illiter-
ate charm. What is he, a blond Adonis? Does
he talk to his surfboard?"

"He's a dark-haired Adonis."

"Uh-oh. I'm telling you, they get you with
that baby-faced charm and then they rape you.
At midnight. He knows you're alone too. Listen,
I'm being serious."

"This one's no rapist," Trisha said. "He's very
nice. He has some troubles."

"Trisha, grow up. He's playing on your sym-
pathies."

"I don't know, Naomi, between television and
a midnight rape . . ."

"You're being very foolish."

"Scamp will protect me."

"She couldn't protect you from a frog. I want
to come see you. Tonight."

"Make it tomorrow, okay? Don't worry. I
could always call Stu and Stacy. The two of
them could handle him."

"I'll be down the day after tomorrow," Naomi said. "Tomorrow's no good."

Trisha built a fire carefully in the big living-room fireplace and looked on with satisfaction as it caught from a single match. She made herself a mug of tea and stretched out on the big couch that was covered in a nubby cotton. She had supervised the building of the house and had chosen every piece of furniture in it, and as she lay there she was pleasantly conscious of the big room with its high ceilings and bookcases. The house was easily heated and stayed cool under an August sun. There was something about having all this comfort and space and knowing at the same time that the beach and the sea lay just beyond the great windows. A wind was rising and the sea, now a battleship gray, showed whitecaps. Trisha felt snug and picked up her book with what she thought was contentment.

But she could not concentrate. She found herself thinking about Strip, wondering if he had gone back to town. Or was he in his car on the highway or still on the beach? Probably he wouldn't hang around for long, with the weather changing. He had an intelligent, sensitive face, though his language was not exactly polished. He was rather quick to take offense. What was he doing here? She could not believe he actually had friends with a Malibu house. Where would he have met them? His friends would be street kids like himself, living on—she hardly knew what. Selling dope and parking cars. Stealing. But Strip didn't act like a criminal, except maybe for his constant line of chatter, the way he tried to ingratiate himself. But he didn't appear to be trying to put anything over on her. All he had done was to give her four little pills. *Stolen* pills.

To distract herself she reached over to the remote control and switched on the TV, a large screen built into the bookshelves. Soap operas. Game shows. An old William Holden spy movie. She was about to settle for that when there was a loud knock at the front door. Scamp ran to investigate. Another knock.

Trisha went to the door and, without opening it, asked who was there.

"It's Pizza Man!"

"You've got the wrong house."

"Come on. Can't you take a joke? It's me. Strip. Listen, did I leave my T-shirt there?"

"Yes. I'll get it."

"Can't I come in? It's cold out here."

"Stay there. I'll get it." She started to look around, not remembering what she had done with it.

"Let me in. Come on. If it was a delivery boy you'd let him in."

"Not if you were the delivery boy, I wouldn't. Go around to the deck. I think it's out there."

By the time she got to the back of the house Strip was peering through the windows at her.

"I don't see it," he mouthed and gestured through the window.

She tried to show some exasperation but was conscious that she didn't feel all that exasperated. She opened the back door, saw the shirt immediately over in a corner, and pointed to it. Scamp hurried out to leap on Strip.

"Thanks," he said. "It's my favorite one. Jeez, this dog is crazy about me." He grinned up at Trisha, playfully shoving at Scamp.

"Come on in, Scamp," Trisha said.

"Wait a minute," Strip said. "Could I ask you a question?"

"No. Good-bye. That's all you do is ask questions. Come on, Scamp." The dog stayed with Strip.

"I'm sorry," Strip said, scratching Scamp between the ears. "If my friends were here I wouldn't be such a pain." He sat down on the steps with the dog.

"If they're not here," Trisha said, "why don't you go home?"

"My car broke down." He sneezed and sniffled. "It's about as dependable as my friends." He sneezed again. "What a world!"

Trisha was staring at him. "How come you look at me like I'm lying all the time?" Strip asked. His face was open.

"Why do you look like you're lying?" Trisha said. The remark was just a comeback. As she said it, she knew she didn't believe it. At that moment, Strip appeared to have about as much guile as Scamp. "Scamp, come here," Trisha called, slapping her knee. She felt a bit guilty for being so cold to Strip. When he put his head in his arms and sneezed hard enough to make Scamp jump, Trisha felt even worse.

"Why don't you put a sweater on?" she said.

"Somebody swiped my backpack." He

clenched his fists. "I'd like to get my hands on the creep-geek who stole it! Shit. Excuse my language."

Trisha found herself moving toward him. "It's just a backpack," she said quietly, repressing an impulse to give him a soothing stroke across his black hair.

But Strip turned on her. "Just a backpack! Look, losin' my backpack is like if somebody came into this place and cleaned you out lock, stock, and barrel! How would you feel? You can't even understand, can you? Imagine all your hundred and fifty dresses and rings and everything ripped off in one swoop. Hell, you can't even imagine. You probably got another house and closetsful of clothes and insurance and God knows what shit. Look, I don't happen to have even one other backpack so don't give me no 'Aww, it's just a backpack.'" After his outburst, his anger dissipated in another big sneeze.

The sound of the telephone kept Trisha from answering him. As she went inside, Strip decided to clear out. He got up to go, but Scamp persuaded him to a farewell pat on the head. Then he noticed that the telephone was still ringing. Surely Trisha would have had time to answer it by now, but she was letting it ring. Finally it stopped, and Strip waited a bit to see whether she would come out again. When she didn't, he started down the stairs.

But before he reached the beach Trisha was calling to him. She stood carrying a blanket and a sweater and a tray with a sandwich and a glass of orange juice on it. Strip watched her put everything down and beckon to him. He didn't know what to say. His throat tightened. Trisha could see his emotion and she silently thanked God that for once she hadn't been uptight and suspicious of him. He came back up the steps and sat down before his food, silently.

"Put this one," she said, handing him the sweater. He pulled it over his head and started on the sandwich, finding it difficult to swallow.

"Take these with the juice," Trisha said, handing him two pills.

"So now you're making me a pill-head!" Strip laughed. He was glad to have something to joke about. "I never seen these kinds."

"It's just vitamin C and an antihistamine."

"Boy, what a disappointment."

"Take them, silly."

"How about some reds so I can sleep?" He sneezed hard.

Trisha moved toward him and placed her hand on his forehead. He stopped chewing and held his breath and found himself pressing his head against her hand.

"Take the pills," Trisha said. He did, looking at her. They stared at each other.

Suddenly Strip took Trisha's hand. "Maybe I should sleep inside," he said. "Where it's really warm. Nip the thing in the bud. So I won't get the flu. Right?" Trisha tried to pull away, but he held her.

"You're not even hot," she said.

"Yeah? Then let me come in 'cause I'm so cold." He let her go and pulled the blanket around his shoulders, shivering.

"Why do you make me doubt you? What a con artist!"

Strip threw the blanket down angrily. He felt his forehead. "You're sure I don't feel hot? You're so sure? I feel cold, the fact is. Like a corpse. What does that mean? What does big nurse have to say about that? Should I drop dead?"

"You'll survive," Trish said evenly, starting toward the door. "Finish eating. And just leave the tray on the table, please."

Strip tossed the remains of the sandwich aside and got up. He glared at her.

"No, thanks! I will not eat another bite. Listen, you know why you doubt me? Because you're naturally suspicious, that's why. I never met a rich person who wasn't. How come you don't get an electric fence around this place? You oughta mine the beach, keep meetin' up with a crude type like me. Well, I got my doubts about your type too. I've had plenty of experience with people like you and it was all lousy. Take the food and take your blanket back. You probably thought I'd sell it. I'm mad I even took those pills."

He stomped down the stairs and, remembering the sweater, pulled it off violently and threw it back.

"Strip," Trisha said, "take the sweater. You've too much false pride."

"So! Now even my pride is false! That's really the end. A nice boy like me with false pride." Then he hurried away.

That night Trish needed another pill to sleep.

Maybe I ought to take a course in human relations, she thought. She didn't know what to think about Strip. Not much seemed to be going right in her life.

Six

Six

TRISHA drove along the Coast Highway at a good clip. She was headed for the market and had made out a careful shopping list, determined to keep things in order. It was almost noon, and that morning she had awakened early, in spite of the pill, and had had coffee and orange juice on the deck. She had half expected Strip would come by again on some pretense. After all, she had managed to insult him one way or another every time they had talked, and there was no reason to believe that he would not come back. She didn't know whether she found him an amusement or a bother. She supposed he was at least a diversion from books and television, and she had caught herself worrying about him from time to time, when she wasn't worrying about herself. Whatever Naomi said, Trisha found it hard to imagine Strip as a threat, unless he was the world's greatest actor, in which case he was really wasting his time selling pills.

Suddenly there he was by the side of the road, rummaging in the trunk of a beat-up old Firebird. She remembered that he had said that his car had broken down. At least now she knew that was true. She managed to pull over and get out without his noticing her. She watched him poking around and muttering to himself. What a character.

67

"Hello," she said. He glanced at her for a second and turned away.

"I suppose it must shock you," he said, "finding such a nice boy like me with his car broken down. You think I'd have the sense to have a car that wouldn't break down. Thing is, I have this policy. I only let my mechanic work on it once every five years. Saves time and money. I was overdue for a check up by twenty-four hours and look what happens. That'll teach me to be punctual."

"I'm sorry if I offended you yesterday," Trisha said. "You have to understand. We have such different backgrounds."

"You're telling me? That's okay. I'm very broadminded."

"Are you a member of the auto club?"

"Do I look like a member of the auto club? That's what I mean! It isn't even my car, it's Greggie's. I was going to sell it and get bail for him. Now, shit."

He was bending over going through some tools in the trunk, and Trisha noticed his nice round butt. Lucky fellow, she thought, surprising herself.

"I'll call Triple-A and have them pick up the car," Trisha said. "I really am sorry about yesterday. I don't want to hurt your feelings. You're right, Strip. I'm suspicious of everything."

Strip straightened up without responding and went around to lift up the hood.

"You followin' me?" he said. "I'll call the cops."

Trisha found herself feeling confident and warm toward him. She sensed that, for some reason, there was a pleasant bond between them now and all she had to do was tug on it, gently.

"What're you after now?" Strip asked as Trisha moved toward him.

"Well, first of all I want you to come have lunch with me while they fix the car."

"I'm frightened," he said. "I think you're carrying a gun in your purse."

"Come on," she asid. She reached out and took his hand. She held it firmly and led him to her car. "Get in," she said.

She could feel him looking at her as she drove back to her house. She was not sorry he was looking at her, because she felt good, full of life as she had not for a long while. She pushed in a cassette.

"How old are you?" she asked, very bold. He didn't answer. He was slumped over on his side of the car and she noticed a grin, a rather shy, embarrassed grin on his face that he tried to hide with his hand. "What are you doing with your life?" she asked.

"What are you doing with yours?"

As they entered the tall double doors at the front of the beach house, Strip was tempted to comment on how much trouble he had had getting his foot inside, but he did not. He was feeling her friendliness too keenly for sarcasm, and he was immediately taken aback by the size, grandeur, and opulence of the place. On the right as they entered was a glassed-in atrium with a huge redwood hot-tub, and inside the ceilings seemed to soar above the comfortable furniture and the books and paintings. He thought of his own dumpy, smelly room and wondered what he would have to do and how long it would take to afford a place like this. Obviously, people who lived this way didn't have to think about the cost at all. What in hell did her house in town look like? This was just a weekend shack! Trisha had disappeared into the kitchen and he found himself staring at a row of fat books in brightly colored jackets. He had an impulse to pull one off the shelf, just to have something to do, but he didn't want to mess them up. Christ, he thought. An alarm would probably go off. He was about to push a button on the TV remote control when Trisha appeared carrying a bottle of wine and a corkscrew.

"Why don't you go out on the deck and open this," she said. "Everything's okay with your car. Just relax while I fix us something."

By the time Trisha emerged on the deck, pushing a wheeled cart, Strip had managed to extract half the cork and to push the other half down into the wine.

"This is the weirdest damned corkscrew . . ."

"Don't worry about it," Trisha said. "I do that all the time."

She got a strainer and poured glasses of red wine. She held up her glass and touched it gently to Strip's. "Please just relax," she said. "Don't make so much of everything. I know I've been acting stupidly." They drank together, and Trisha served them from a large glass bowl.

"What's this?" Strip asked, staring at his food.

"Salade Nicoise."

"Oh, yeah? You don't say. Looks like tuna fish to me. Hey, whadda ya know, tastes like tuna fish too. I'll be damned."

Trisha was amused by the friendly little battle that was going on now. She wanted him to like her food and he was determined not to be intimidated by it. She was getting used to his flip-flops from being defensive to being aggressive, the rhythm of his personality. She liked it.

"This house," Strip said. "You build it or what?"

"We have an architect who's a friend."

I'll bet he got paid anyway, Strip thought. He stared at Trisha and she looked desirable to him. She was wearing a dark Greek sweater and white slacks and, whatever her age, she looked alive and elegant and reminded him of pictures of jetsetters and movie stars, lounging at some resort. She had high color from the beach and the way she sat, legs crossed with one arm draped casually over the back of her chair, the wine held gracefully by the glass's stem, made him admire her. She took a sip and the wine colored her lips.

"Why were you suspicious of me?" Strip asked.

"I don't know. I lead a sheltered life."

"Yeah. I'll bet you thought I was gonna try and rip you off."

"No. I don't know what I thought."

"Maybe I am. This is some place you got here. Maybe I just wanna con you enough so's you'll look the other way when I scarf up all your furs and jewels."

71

"Maybe I wouldn't care."

Scamp broke the mood. She hurled herself onto the deck sopping wet, caked with sand. I hadn't even noticed she was gone, Trisha thought. "Where have you been, you bad dog! I'll have to take you to the groomer's now!"

"Don't waste your money," Strip said. "Let me do it. Where's her brush? Hey, you can trust me. When I get through with her she'll be ready for a fashion show."

Trisha got him the brush and went to answer the phone, hoping it wouldn't be Stu. It was Naomi, calling from Elizabeth Arden's where she was having everything imaginable done to herself.

"Just a sec, Trish," Naomi said, sounding frantic. "Katrina, not so hot, for God's sake. Last time I fainted dead away."

"Call me later, Naomi. I'm in the middle of something."

"You are? Wait. I've got to tell you. I was at Scandia. I had the stuffed trout, you know? Well. Guess who I saw." Trisha didn't respond. "I'll tell you who. Stacy."

"So?"

"Who do you think she was with?"

"Stu. So what?"

"Trisha! What kind of a friend do you think I am? Do you think—ouch! My God, why do I put myself through this torture!—so you think I'd call to torture you with that? No, darling, she was having lunch with Dan Santini!"

"I'm sorry, Naomi, but what possible interest do you think I might have in that piece of startling information?"

"Well, for one thing, it means she wasn't having lunch with Stu. And after all, you know what Dan Santini is. And he's just dumped his latest mistress. Didn't you hear that?"

"No."

"Of course not. You don't know anything that's going on in this town. That's why I'm so invaluable to you darling. What would you do without me?"

"I know you're invaluable, Naomi, but to tell you the truth, I just can't be all that concerned with all that business. One thing I'm beginning to realize: I have to work things out for myself. I have to act on my own. Eventually Stu will figure out what he wants to do and then we can see what happens. Until then he's got to go his way and I'm going mine."

"That sounds terribly dramatic."

Strip entered the house cradling Scamp wrapped in a towel. He came over to Trisha. "Guess what?" he said. "Scamp's got a friend. Come see."

"Well," Naomi said. "I can see you *are* going your own way. Who is he? The beach boy you told me about? Oh my God."

"Don't jump to conclusion, Naomi. I'll have to talk to you later. Thanks for calling. See you soon." She hung up.

Outside she found a little black-and-white mutt waiting for Scamp. Strip put Scamp down and the dogs chased each other around, but Trisha noticed that the mutt had a bad hind leg. She went over to examine him. He had no collar, had obviously been wandering around homeless, and licked her hand as though he'd come home at last.

"You sure do like animals," Strip said. "I though you'd turn up your nose at this swamp toad. He ain't got much class."

"Scamp's usually the one who turns up her nose."

"He's got a bum leg."

"I can see that. Did you bite him, Scamp?"

"Naw," Strip said. "I'll bet he got hit by a car. I don't think it's broken, though. Hey, could I use your phone? I gotta make a call real bad. It's urgent."

"Of course. You don't have to ask. Just go ahead."

Trisha thought Strip seemed suddenly very nervous. He was looking around as though he expected someone to sneak up on him. She asked him whether he was in some sort of trouble.

"I'll be straight with you," he said, pausing in the doorway. "I sincerely don't know whether I'm in trouble or not. I've been afraid to go home, to tell you the truth. But the trouble is Greggie. When they find out he's busted—these people don't play around, see? I think I gotta go into town and see what's comin down."

Trisha followed him inside and started tidying up the kitchen as he dialed. But, with profuse apologies, he asked whether she would mind if the call were private.

"Of course not," she said, and added on impulse, "I'll call my lawyer for you if you want, Strip, as soon as you get off."

"That's fantastic!" he said. "I didn't want to

ask you, but—that means a lot. Okay, let me make my call."

While Strip was on the phone, Trisha had second thoughts. She had acted out of spontaneous generosity, but did she really want to get herself and her lawyer involved in this mess? He probably didn't even handle criminal cases. He would send them to someone else, and who would pay for it all? Well, she would. But my God, this Greggie might be a real lost cause.

When Strip got off the phone he was pale and anxious. He said he had to get into town and would leave as soon as his car was fixed.

"They said it'd be ready by now," Trisha said. "What about calling my lawyer?"

"No need for that now," Strip said. "Greggie's out on bail."

"Wonderful!" Trisha said.

"No, it ain't. See you later." He started off, but Trisha made him let her drive him. She wondered how he was involved and was not sure whether she wanted to know. It was upsetting. For a few moments everything had been peaceful between them.

"What kind of trouble are you in?" Trisha asked. She was driving toward the garage, keeping below the speed limit, hoping to get at least part of the story before she dropped him off.

"It's more like I don't know," Strip said. "I gotta find out, and I gotta make sure Greggie is okay."

"I wish you wouldn't be so mysterious. He's out of jail, isn't he? What have you done? Are the police after you for stealing pills?"

"It's the guys running the operation. You never know what they're thinkin'. You gotta stay on top of 'em, you know? They like to settle things quick."

"What guys?" Trisha asked. "Mobsters? You're not tangled up with organized crime?"

"They're pretty well organized, all right. Let me brush your hair back. It's in your eyes."

She ran her hand through her hair. "Why would they have it in for you?" she asked. Trisha was far from naive about the criminal element in business. She didn't like to discuss it with Stu because she knew there was nothing she could do about it, but she was aware of pay-offs and phony bank accounts. She knew what sort of connections a man like Dan Santini had, and, living in a town that was the center of the entertainment industry, you had to be a fool not to have some ideas of tie-ins among Las Vegas, Hollywood, and Wall Street. But Strip wasn't in that league. If he had criminal associations, they must be pretty lowdown.

"It's not really me." Strip sighed. "I been strictly Mickey Mouse. It's Greggie. He was in real tight. He's a genius for makin' pills, see. I mean, the guy oughta go to work for some company, but you know how it is. He ain't got no degree. Shit, he ain't even finished high school. Nobody'd hire him. So these guys, they let him work in their lab. He knows too much."

"Didn't he work at Schwab's?"

"Sure. They got him that. A front. And he was coppin' quinine, procaine, stuff like that. I don't know the whole story."

"So what are you worried about?" Trisha

asked. "I know you're concerned about your friend, but *he's* the one in trouble. You haven't done anything."

"Christ. You don't know much, do you? Don't you see, they know him and me is buddies. It's obvious they sprung Greggie. If they leave him alone now, we're both all right. But if they worry he's gonna start talkin', we're both in trouble. See, they don't even know what I don't know. I'll be honest with you. If I was in their place, I'd be worryin' too. Only one way for 'em to stop worryin'. It's a tried and true method." He took a deep breath. "Somehow I gotta convince 'em they can trust us."

"Strip, I don't think you should make any contact with those people at all. And I think you should let Greggie take care of himself. If you're not really that involved, it's not up to you to sacrifice yourself."

"Me and Greggie, we have our disagreements, but we're together. He'd do the same for me."

"You've got to make your own way in the world. Otherwise you can't help anybody."

"Just like you, huh? Making your own way in the world."

The pointed reference to her husband's money silenced Trisha. Strip tried to explain, gently, that he didn't really have a choice. He had to do something to protect Greggie, and he couldn't just pretend that he wasn't involved. Maybe it was tough for her to understand, but outside her world it wasn't so easy to keep from having contact with people who were less than a hundred percent legitimate. Maybe even her husband hadn't made all his money strictly on the up and up. It just wasn't possible. And for a guy like himself, without even a high school education, with nobody to help him get started, he had to take what he could get. Within limits.

"I gotta find a way to work with 'em," he said, "to protect Greggie. The only thing, if I had somethin' they wanted and they couldn't get it except by dealin' with me. I don't know."

"I'm sure you'll find a way to impress them," Trisha said, her voice heavy with disapproval.

"Hey, don't worry about me. I been on my own since I was fourteen, you know. It ain't like I don't know the score."

"Have you been in jail?"

"Me? Naw, I stay clean. Got busted for pot once."

"You did?"

"Yeah. I was growin' my own and dealin' some. Nothin' much. I got off."

"How?"

"Never mind. I'll tell you sometime. Hey, there's the car."

Strip pretended to inspect the engine while Trisha paid the bill. He was embarrassed and grateful at the same time.

She watched him get into the car and grin as it started right up. If he were Tim, she thought, I'd raise hell. But he's not Tim, and he's not anybody with parents and money to back him up. He's on his own. As much as she rejected what he was about to do, she couldn't help admiring his loyalty to his friend. She gave him a little wave, feeling like an army wife or mother or both, sending someone into battle. She felt very anxious for him and hoped he could tell that.

"Hey, Miss Fabulash!" he called. "Thanks for everything!" Then he roared off.

Seven

Seven

STRIP had called a friend of his in the L.A. County Sheriff's Department who had promised to try to see that no harm came to Greggie in jail and to keep track of him. Strip had been calling the friend regularly since he had learned of Greggie's arrest, and each time he telephoned, Strip had been afraid that he would learn that Greggie had been killed or beaten up. Now the news was that he had been bailed out, and Strip feared the worst. If only he had been able to get a high-class lawyer right away, the guy might have been able to spring Greggie and arrange to protect him. Might have.

If he was all right, Greggie would probably head for their apartment. Strip had phoned there too. There had been no answer, but Greggie might have been letting the phone ring. Another might have. Strip was anxious, and he headed straight for the apartment.

It was a long drive. There was no freeway directly to that part of Hollywood from the beach, and as Strip drove through the expensive neighborhoods of the west side he thought of Trisha, who had turned out to be in his corner after all, as much as she could understand his way of life. He had not been foolish to seek her out. She had wanted to help, eventually. And by the time she had, he had grown attached to her. He found her presence reassuring. It was not just her house and money. She was having her problems too, and he admired the way she was dealing with them, keeping her cool, not acting hysterical. It was a wonder that with all she had on her mind, she had given the time of day to him. It just went to show that you could find decent people everywhere, no matter how much money they had. Of course, they were the exceptions.

It was only a room, maybe the cheapest in Los Angeles. He and Greggie paid twenty dollars a week for it, and it was overpriced. Way up on the 1600 block of North Western Avenue, it was the center of what could hardly be called a neighborhood, more a collection of buildings distinguished by their air of imminent collapse. Nothing but pawn shops, porno shops, bars, motels with hourly rates, and a few old fleabag hotels like the La Paula, which Strip called home, the place to go if you want to meet a wino. In L.A. they have a way of tearing down these places before they get to looking that way, but the La Paula had survived, a relic that had no chance at all of being declared a historical landmark.

Strip ran up the stairs to his room, breathing in the familiar urine smell, vaulting over an old man lolling in his vomit. Through his door Strip could hear the telephone ringing, and he hurried with the key. Greggie? Maybe somebody checking up on him. Maybe somebody checking up on me, thought Strip. He was not certain how closely the organization connected him with his friend. If he answered, they could send someone to greet him on his way out.

The ringing stopped before he could get to the phone. He looked around at his room. No sign of Greggie. The room seemed tiny after the beach house: tiny and rotting. A hundred anxious nights sweated through there, when he had lain awake wondering how to get money, what to plan on, where to go next, rushed in on him. Just being away from it for a couple of nights had given him a renewed distaste for it. The yellow-brown walls were brightened by a few rock and country-western posters, James Taylor, Jim Croce, Johnny Cash, and the lyrics of "Bad, Bad Leroy Brown" ran through his head.

Strip tried to decide what to do next. He could not stay there indefinitely. If something had happened to Greggie . . .

He dialed his friend at the sheriff's department. As soon as he hung up, he threw his few things into a suitcase and bolted.

At the beach, Trish had discovered Strip's address book only a few minutes earlier. As she picked it up, a photograph fell out, two kids with their arms around each other, smiling and clowning. Strip and, Trisha guessed, Greggie. A newspaper clipping pressed into the book caught her eye: an ad for a disc jockey school. Employment guaranteed, meet giants of the recording industry, set sights on stardom.

Strip's name, address, and telephone number were neatly inscribed on the inside front cover. She was tempted to call him, because she was extremely worried about him. She rang, but there was no answer.

Trisha, dressed in her caftan, moved about the house, pointlessly tidying up. She had no appetite, she didn't want a drink. She gazed out the window and saw the two dogs frolicking on the beach, the stray limping badly. His injury appeared worse. She would have to take him to the vet in the morning. But the point was, what was she going to do tonight? She felt unaccountably lonely. Yet she dreaded hearing the telephone: It would be either Stu or Naomi. Strip didn't know her number, and it was unlisted. She had a crazy impulse to call information and instruct them to give the number out to any young man identifying himself as Strip. She tried the television news, flipping back and forth between Cronkite and Chancellor, finding both equally uninspiring. She thumbed through three or four magazines, wondering what on earth anyone could find in them. Even Bach, rolling a rich and elevated order through the sound system, seemed stale and flat. A walk was the only thing.

Along the beach she strolled, the dogs running ahead, falling behind, catching up. Lights went on in the other houses along the shore and she smelled barbecues in the sea air, heard voices lubricated with cocktails, observed a couple in their fifties seated on their porch, gins in hands, staring out at the water, not speaking. She reached the rocks at the north end of the beach and tried to take an interest in the tide that fed pools alive with anemones and hermit crabs: life. Did anemones sleep? If Strip appeared again on my doorstep, she thought, I would let him in.

And of course he did appear. He had debated with himself, had bought a half-gallon of Gallo's finest Rhine wine—$2.79—and had mulled over his options, parked along the Coast Highway, swilling and mulling, until the bottle was half gone and he had the courage to face it. He had two options, or so he concluded. He could drive as far as the three dollars he had left would take him, or he could throw himself on her mercy. As he sat drinking, fending off thoughts of Greggie, he felt the awful emptiness of his life, felt a fool to have no one to turn to but this woman he hardly knew. Why didn't he have the resources to solve his problems himself? Other people did. He would end up like the derelict drunks at the La Paula. He drove to a spot near Trisha's house and drank some more. All right, he thought, I will rip her off. She's been so goddamed suspicious, I'll give her something to be suspicious about. I'll con her into letting me in that fucking mansion of hers and I'll grab everything I can get my hands on and split. I'll grab her too, pay her off good for letting me sleep out in the cold. He imagined himself tearing at Trisha's clothes and forcing her down. The thought didn't please him, and he was overcome with shame. She was a nice woman, a really nice woman, and he admired her, the way she was able to cope with things on her own. Maybe she would teach him how to get his own life in order. If only he could talk to her, spill everything out.

Cradling his precious bottle, he made his way unsteadily to the spot between houses where he had watched her the other night, and he drank again, hunkering, taking great gulps of the wine, trying to get up his courage and keep down his pride, his thoughts whirling between Greggie and Trisha. He started to weep and cursing, stopped himself. Then he saw her, wandering back to the house with the dogs. Immediately he moved toward her, stumbling.

"Hey, Miss Mercedes! Hey! Have some um my wine! Hey! Wine! Goddamn!"

What Trisha saw was a small, dark, lurching figure, gesticulating with a big bottle, and only the word wine reached her across the sand. What a disappointment, she thought. She did not have enormous sympathy for drunks. She turned toward the house.

"Wait! Hey, Miss Ultra-frost. What's the matter now? What'd I do now, for chrissakes?"

"I don't like your coming here drunk."

"Drunk? You outa your mind? I have a little wine an' I'm drunk? So is that it? Jesus!"

"You left your address book here. I'll get it."

"Sure, that's why I'm here. I need it. Gotta have it. You know?"

Trisha started up the steps.

"Can I please have permission to use your water? It would maybe help sober me up."

She went inside. Scamp followed her, but the stray dog remained with Strip, who had collapsed on the sand. He felt too heavy to move, but somehow he struggled out of his pants and crawled toward the water, putting his face into it, splashing himself, and then rising and hurtling into the surf. He didn't swim but let himself be rolled around by the gentle waves. When he got out, he was trembling from the effects of cold water and alcohol, and he wondered what he would do now. There was still the address book. He climbed up the sun deck steps, a shivering, dripping waif, the stray dog tagging after him.

"You've had too much to drink." Trisha was not exactly hospitable.

"I just want my address book. That's all I'm here for."

"You're a mess. I'll get it."

She brought him a towel and a blanket, and when he reached for them and mumbled thanks, she told him to dry himself off and get warm and then please go away. He fumbled and dropped the book as she tried to hand it to him. The photograph slipped out. He went to his knees to gather everything up.

But he did not get up. The photograph of himself and Greggie looked up at him from the deck and he felt too weak to rise. There they were together, happy and cocky, full of that adolescent bravado that says to hell with the future. At first Trisha thought he was simply too loaded to get up. Then she noticed tears streaming from his eyes.

"What is it?"

"Nothing."

"Tell me. Come on, I'll listen."

"Greggie's dead."

"Oh, my God. Oh, Strip." She dropped down beside him and held him tight. Then it broke, great sobs, all that had been held back, the sadness and the confusion, swelling out of him in a flood. She held his head and pressed it to her, stroking his wet hair, trying to steady his racked body.

"I'm sorry."

"Don't."

"What a world."

"Yes. What a world."

Then they were silent, his last sobs spending themselves, until they couldn't help noticing the two dogs climbing on them and nuzzling, anxious to get in on the affection, and this made them laugh a little.

"See?" Strip said. "They got problems too."

"Come inside, sweetheart," Trisha said, the word slipping involuntarily from her. "You're freezing. I've got a nice fire."

She led him to the couch by the fire and made him take off his sopping T-shirt and dried him with a towel, rubbing his hair and chest and back. He was still dazed, groggy, but Trisha was very much alert, conscious of him, feeling minglings of impulses, wanting to care for him but wanting to touch him too, his boy's lean body, his man's body, the smooth flesh and the rough, dark beard, the soft dark hairs on him. His eyes were half closed, his head nodding. She fetched a quilt and wrapped it around him, settling him back on the couch. Then she gathered up his wet shirt and laid it out before the fire, adding another log. The wood flared up.

"Don't go away," came his small voice from the couch.

"I'm not going anywhere. I'm right here."

"Where are you?"

"Let me turn out the lights."

By firelight she came back to him, sat down by him, and cradled him in her arms.

"Don't leave me."

"I'm right here. I'll hold you."

Eight

MORNING. They lay side by side on the couch, Strip still sleeping, Trisha on the inside with her arms around him, awake and welcoming first light. She had held him all night, because she wanted to and because, she thought warmly, affectionately, and with some little amusement, he might fall off otherwise; held him with his head nestled into her shoulder, her body against his, her legs entangled with his. She had dozed off a couple of times but had been awake most of the night watching the fire die and holding him, breathing with him, and now she saw the dawn spreading slowly, calmly, a morning blessing. She felt that she was blessed and she put her lips to his ear, thinking, Good morning, sweet Strip, looking down at his dark arm curled up under his chin. She breathed in his smell, sea-salt and the faint odor of wine, not unpleasant, and some other, human, male smell. She put her hand deliberately on his bare side, tracing with her fingers his gently moving ribs.

He stirred, turned, and looked into her eyes. No hesitation now. As if it had been inevitable from the start they kissed, and Trisha felt herself melt. He was on his back and she moved over onto him, raising herself to let his arms go around her, then lowering herself. And instantly she could feel him, so hard, so insistently hard and full it was a shock, and from deep in her throat came a joyous, shocked sigh of pleasure.

Easily he lifted her caftan, started to kiss her breasts, free moons over him, but she didn't want to wait or play, she wanted him, and in a single, certain movement she raised and lowered herself, and they were one. For a while he lay still as she took from him. Then he began to buck and thrash, and she looked down at him with greedy pleasure. They stole looks into each other's eyes, frank in the morning light, open, woman and boy, man and woman, two made one, their desires feeding each other, one body moving of itself, delighting in itself, melting, finally into itself. Then they rolled onto their sides and for a long time held each other, still one, neither moving nor speaking.

Of the two, Trisha felt the more peaceful and fulfilled, while Strip, though he was conscious of having experienced the most intense of pleasures, was a little unnerved, a little uncertain, so different had it been, so strange to him the part he had played—unaggressive, almost passive, yet excited beyond thought. It was almost as though she had fucked him, and not the other way around. He had been with girls who had not hidden their excitement, but this had been something different—and then he stopped wondering and worrying as Trisha kissed him so tenderly, so fully, that he felt himself growing excited again and again they made love, side by side this time, and he pressed into her as though he were trying to disappear.

Coffee and oranges moved the day another moment forward. Strip wanted to make himself useful. He repaired the broken fixture. He drove to the drugstore and bought ointment and bandages for the stray dog. Trisha watched with admiration as he cleaned the wound, which had begun to abscess, dressed it, bandaged it. He knew what he was doing.

"I think we have a new dog," he said. "He'll never leave now."

"I wonder where he came from. He must belonged to somebody sometime."

"Hold this while I tape it."

Trisha knelt to help. Strip seemed lost in what he was doing, intent but a little sad. Had she done something wrong? "You must have belonged to someone sometime," she said.

"Why? Me and the stray, we're on our own."

She took his hand and asked him to talk to her, tell her about himself, but he was moody, withdrawn, sighing a lot, pulling away from her. She held him, moved nearer to him on the rug.

"Why did you leave home?"

"I felt like it."

"Tell me. I want to know. I care about you."

"I had a dog when I was a kid. Name of Corky."

"Then that's what we'll call this one," Trish said. "Corky."

Corky hobbled around.

"Will he be all right, do you think?"

"Sure," Strip said.

"Will you?"

"Sure." He got up and looked out the window. "Maybe I'll go swimmin'."

She offered to call her lawyer about Greggie,

but Strip just shrugged, as though calling a lawyer about a dead man seemed pretty pointless. Trisha, giving up trying to make him talk, came up behind him and put her arms around him. She raised his hair off his neck and kissed him there. She felt his breathing quicken and whispered to him to go swimming; she would have lunch ready when he came back. She felt tension drain from him and turned him around, holding him by the shoulders.

"What would you like?"

"Something besides tuna fish."

They laughed, hugged each other, and she could tell he wanted to make love again. Not that she didn't feel it too, but she instinctively thought they should go slowly, thought he needed to regain a sense of himself.

"I thought you wanted to go swimming."

"I didn't want to, you know, talk."

"You go on. Then we'll eat, and we can talk then, if you want to."

She cooked hamburgers on the grill and served them on a platter with big slices of Bermuda onion. They ate on the deck.

"This is fantastic."

"Just hamburgers."

"No. Give me some more wine. God, I never thought I'd drink wine again."

"The human body has amazing powers of recovery. Haven't you noticed?"

He leaned over to kiss her, but she pushed him gently away. "Not here. People might see. Don't forget I'm a respectable married woman."

"I noticed that, yeah. Hey, you got a pencil?"

He folded over a paper napkin and wrote

something on it, then stuffed it into the empty wine bottle, replacing the cork.

"I'm sending a message."

He took the bottle down to the water and flung it like a discus beyond the breaker line. Trisha came down onto the sand and they sat watching the bottle float out. She wondered what the message was but felt he would tell her if he wanted to. A call for help? A prayer? People who sent messages in bottles were stranded on desert islands, shipwrecked. It fit.

"Strip, let me help. Tell me about yourself. Don't you trust me now? Tell me what really happened with Greggie. How you got mixed up."

"Who says I was mixed up? Look, I don't mean this in a bad way, see, but to tell you the truth, you don't understand nothin'. You gonna have much trouble paying the rent this month? What the hell, you don't even have rent, do you?"

"No. We have a mortgage."

"Sure. Well, if you're gonna see it at all, you gotta put yourself in my shoes. I mean, I got nothin', nothin' at all. I don't say it'll always be this way. I got confidence. I can make it. But I ain't made it yet. No way."

"The thing you mustn't do is think you have to get mixed up with a lot of criminals to make it."

"Oh, yeah? Sure, that's the right thing to say, but you try living on the street for a while and you'll begin to see you can't afford to make such nice distinctions. Besides, the way I see it, you wanna move, you got to take what comes along. There ain't no other way."

"Just explain to me what happened with Greggie."

A little condescendingly, like teacher to pupil, Strip laid out the scene for her. A big drug sweep had been rumored. Once Greggie had been caught, his number was up. He already had one conviction, and obviously the organization figured he would cooperate with the police rather than be sent up for ten years. They had killed him, made it look as though he had o.d.'d.

"What about you?"

"I wasn't that involved," Strip said. "I got a sense of preservation. I know if you know too much, you're a target. I kept tellin' Greggie not to get in so tight with those guys, but he didn't listen. He probably thought I was jealous."

"They won't be after you?"

"I doubt it. I panicked at first but when I think about it, they don't give a shit about me probably. Still, you never know. They can be pretty thorough."

"It all sounds like a movie."

"Maybe you should believe more what you see in the movies."

They fell silent. Trisha began putting some suntan lotion on herself, gestured with it toward him, and went around behind him to put some on his back.

"That's good. You better put some on my front, too."

"I think you'd better."

"Hey, come on. You gettin' uptight again?

You got me to talk. It's the least you could do."

"Then keep talking."

"You keep rubbin', I'll keep talking."

She worked around to his chest, then tried to hand the bottle to him, so he could do his legs.

"Come on. You want me to burn?" He lay back and she kept rubbing. His feet; up his legs. "I turn you on, don't I? Admit it."

"You're a runaway. Like Greggie. Why?"

"I ain't no runaway. What a dumb word. I just left home, that's all. I left plenty of clues. My parents could've found me. They didn't try."

She had been leaning over him, rubbing in the lotion, and when she finished she found herself drawn down, kissing him.

"What about the goddamned neighbors?" Strip whispered. "Aw, don't pull away. It's too late now. Your reputation's ruined. Might as well go all out. Trisha."

It was the first time he said her name and the sound of it on his lips made her want to collapse on him, but she sat up slowly.

"I really make you hot," Strip said.

"Why did you leave home?" She formed the words with difficulty, as though she were drunk.

"Christ," he said. "That's a million years ago."

"You should like it that I want to know about you."

She lay back beside him and asked him again about his home, and at last he began to tell her, hesitantly, clearly not really wishing to relieve the past, yet willing to open it to her, as though submitting to what he was for the time being going to accept as her wisdom. And as he talked he was conscious of what he was leaving out.

He had a strange sense that he didn't want to betray his parents, even though he felt they had betrayed him. He told her how he had run off on his fourteenth birthday, September 4th, because they had forgotten about it; how he had waited around all day to see whether they had remembered and that when it had become obvious that there wasn't going to be a present or a cake or anything, he had hit the road. What he hadn't told her was that he had ceased to expect anything like a birthday party and had decided weeks before that when he turned fourteen, that would be it. He lived on Third Street in Riverside, sixty miles east of Los Angeles, the place where all the smog ends up. His block of Third Street was old tract houses, badly built twenty-five years ago and crumbling now, a neighborhood of the lower working class and the unemployed, where having a lawn usually meant whether you mowed the weeds or not and where landscaping meant abandoned cars and pick-ups in the front yard; where in the summer the families that were getting along sat out front drinking beer and the families that weren't getting along stayed inside and beat hell out of one another.

His father had been a steelworker at the Kaiser plant in Fontana in what must have been the good days, before Strip had come along, before his father had been laid off and had begun a series of dead-end jobs—watchman, janitor, car salesman. He had landed a good job in the hardware department at Sears but it hadn't lasted. Strip's brother, eight years older, a Vietnam vet, had been up on a hit-and-run charge and his father had gone into the hole to pay a no-good lawyer who had succeeded in getting the brother two years in Chino prison. From then on, the father went down and down. Strip could remember cowering in his bed, terrified, waiting for his father to come home to beat up his mother. You fat bitch, you no good cunt whore, and then the sounds of cold-cuffing, screaming, pleading, and for days his mother would sit in the house hiding her injuries, watching the soaps. He didn't tell Trisha any of that. It was a kind of loyalty to his mother and father. He couldn't bring himself to blame them for anything. They had simply reached the point where they couldn't think about him any more and there had been nothing for him to do but split or get swallowed up in their misery. He had left, telling himself, as he still did, that he would not let anything like their life happen to him.

"Forget it," Trisha said. "Don't be bitter. Maybe it was a mistake to run away, just because of your birthday."

"I can take a hint. I don't like to stick around where I'm not wanted. You ever notice that about me?"

"I noticed you have a way of making yourself wanted."

He couldn't help grinning.

Trisha asked how he had met Greggie and he recalled how they had hooked up on Highway 60, hitching to L.A., how they had become partners right away.

"Partners in what?"

"Getting by. Making it. Staying alive."

"Aren't you going to call his parents?"

"I gotta work out somethin' to tell 'em. I can't just say Greggie got himself killed—they'd want to know what he was into. I gotta tell 'em he was framed or whatever. Christ. What a world."

He slumped, looking suddenly like an old man with the burdens of generations on his shoulders, ready to give up the ghost. Trisha bent over and kissed him unashamedly, and he kissed back, took her in his arms, moving over onto her. For what seemed a long time she was lost in his intensity, and then she forced herself into consciousness and said, "Not here, inside, let's go inside."

Nine

"LET's get this goop off first," she said.

"Why? It's nice." He reached for her. They were in the living room and Strip was ready to pick up where they had left off that morning.

"I bet you've never been in a hot tub," she said.

"I bet you've never been in a whorehouse. On second thought—"

"Strip! Come on. We'll take a bath together."

"All *right!*"

"Put some music on—that switch over there. I'll start it running."

He pressed the switch and music filled the house. It was not Strip's favorite kind of music, lush strings, movie themes, but he was impressed and imagined what Fleetwood Mac would sound like on this system. He looked around and spotted a family photo, parents and son Tim posed in front of the beachhouse. A good-looking kid, like his mom, Strip thought. He scrutinized Stu, thinking. Wonder what he'd think now. Christ, he's pretty big. Let's hope he doesn't just decide to drop in.

In the atrium near the front door Trisha sat, a towel around her, dangling her legs into the swirling water, and as Strip came up she tossed aside the towel and slipped into the large redwood tub, a slim water nymph, graceful monarch of this place. Strip felt the blood rush to his head and quickly struggled out of his trunks, lowering himself into the water beside her.

"Hey, this is too much. And that sound system you got in there. You always go first class, don'tcha?" He reached for her and she went into his arms. Her slippery body delighted him, and he drew in his breath at the feel of her wet, buoyant breasts against him. "Listen. I done a lot of talkin' but I haven't said what's on my mind, you know?"

"I have some pot. Want to get it?"

"No, I don't. I don't even want a vitamin pill. I don't need nothin' with you. I gotta tell you somethin'."

"What do you want to tell me?" Boldly she put her hands between his legs and held him. "What else is there to say?"

"I love you."

"Of course you do. I can tell. It's so easy to tell, isn't it?" She moved her fingers along him. "You're saying it all. You don't have to say anything. God."

"I'm serious."

"I never felt anything so serious."

"Look." He pulled back from her. "I really mean it, I love you!"

She laughed, and as she did so, felt him shrink.

"Strip? I'm sorry. It's—"

"You got a complete genius for hurting my feelings." He moved farther away from her. Two or three feet of swirling water separated them now. "What's the matter? You think I'm not good enough for you? I'm too low-class, aren't I?"

"That's not true."

"I was good enough for you this morning, all right. Wasn't I? Sure, you love me too. You love me in bed."

"I certainly do. It's true, I love you in bed. A lot. And on the couch. And in here."

"But not out of bed, is that it?"

"What are you saying? Why do you want to spoil this? Of course I love you out of bed. You're the most lovable creature I—"

"Creature. What am I, some kinda dog?"

"Strip, please. I love you in and out of bed. I do."

"Then just say it. Go on. Why won't you admit it? Tell me you love me. Let it all out, you'll feel better."

She moved toward him but he put out his hand to stop her: "Not until you admit you love me."

"I can't believe this. It's ridiculous."

"Ridiculous that we love each other? This is the most feeling I've ever felt before." He waited for a response, but she only stared at him as though he was slightly mad. "Listen, we could really have something together. We're really somethin', don't you see that? I don't mean just sex. I mean everything. You don't know how I feel. I mean, I was so drawn to you. I love your style. What's the matter with you? You want some kind of stud? You want a quick grind? You got the wrong stud. I must've misjudged you."

Trisha backed away from him. "I wish you hadn't put it that way."

"So that's what you want. Goddamn! So

you're nothing but some horny housewife? God-damn? Why don't you just stand out on the highway and lift your skirt!"

"Stop it. You don't know what you're saying."

"You don't want me. All you want is my cock." Furious, he started to hoist himself out of the water. Trisha grabbed his ankle but he shook her off, scrambled out, and grabbed a towel.

"You're impossible!" she shouted. "Don't you realize what a child you're being?"

"Let's not start talking about ages, okay?" He loomed over her. "I'm gonna listen to some music. When you're ready to admit you love me, you can have me. Just like that." He snapped his fingers. "If you're not ready to com-mit yourself, forget it, baby. You got the wrong guy." He moved to the doorway as she turned her back on him and sank in the water to her neck. "It's over, understand? Unless you want what we could have. Something really beauti-ful. I've had it with quickies and cheap, mean-ingless fucking, see? I'm sick of it. You end up with nothing and that's what I've got." He started through the doorway and then stepped back. "Not that I don't feel lucky and grateful and all that, with somebody like you wantin' me. I mean, I'm flattered and all that you want to make it with me, believe me. I've considered myself a lucky guy all my life but I'll be honest with you, I never lucked out like this before. Therefore, I would hate to blow it, believe me. But I'll kiss it good-bye, because the older I get I realize I got to have some principles, and

110

there's an important principle at stake here, even if you can't see it. Do you see it?"

"No, frankly."

"It's—I can't put my finger on it. I can't say what it is. I quit school and I don't talk as good as you, but I can see it and you oughta be able to see it too, a woman like you. I can't believe you don't."

"I've never had cheap sex before. I was sort of looking forward to it. Cheap, unprincipled, immoral, scandalous, passionate, unbridled. Plain lust."

"And you figured I was just the guy. Well, you figured wrong!" he said angrily, rushing out.

Trisha stayed in the tub to soak and think. She was not angry or hurt. She was frustrated, and at the same time a little amused, though she told herself that the last thing she wanted to do was to reveal her amusement to him in the slightest. It would kill him. What a character. Even when he was being most absurd, there was something appealing about. The poor kid, he really needed someone to love him. All his talk of principles. The only principle involved was his insecurity. If he had even an inkling of how sexy he was, he would never feel insecure for the rest of his life. In a year of two he would know it, if he could stay alive till then. In a year or two he will have so many girls hanging on him I wouldn't be able to get near him. Maybe. She let herself float in the tub, trying to relax, to let the heat she felt for him cool. It didn't.

It occurred to her that she was being pretty

111

ludicrous herself. Why wouldn't she tell him she loved him? After all, she did, now. She didn't know whether she would tomorrow. But now she did. I love you, Strip, she said to herself, I love you, I love you, I would do anything for you, I love you.

Strip lay on the couch, a towel around him, listening to the music, wondering whether he was being a fool. But it was true, he was sick of what he had known with girls, tired of being with someone and ending up always alone, tired of waking up in the morning with someone he wanted to get rid of beside him. What he felt for Trisha had become so strong so quickly that he didn't want to risk losing it, cheapening it into a few quick bouts of sex. Maybe he had opened himself up too soon. Maybe you always had to be cagey with women, or you scared them off. Well, this time he didn't care. If he couldn't be open with her and if she couldn't respond in an equal way, it wasn't worth it anyway.

She came into the room wrapped in a white terrycloth robe, her hair black with wet, glowing from the tub's heat, and he wanted her. Wasn't that love written on her face? She stood over him, then lay down beside him, smelling of soap and heat, her robe falling slightly open. Strip fought with himself.

"I don't even know what the word means," she said.

"I'll tell you."

"I don't know what the word love means. I don't know what sex means."

"No?"

"Love."

"Yes?"

"Sex. They're words. They're both nice words. Don't you think?" Her voice embarrassed him, a touch, a soft kiss. She kissed his neck.

"I love you," he said. "I mean it. Sincerely. I can hardly talk I love you so much."

"Don't."

"I never said it to nobody before. Nobody. How many times have you?"

"I don't know. Not enough. Not nearly enough."

"Say it. Make up for it. Now's your chance."

She kissed him endlessly, breathlessly on the mouth, on the neck, and moved her lips to his ear, kissing it.

"Say it," he breathed, moving his hands to her breasts and pushing at them through the cloth, as though to push her away, firmly, and the pressure made her gasp.

"Okay . . . yes," she whispered. "Yes: I love you. I do love you. I love you, I love you."

Ten

THEY had made love all afternoon, tenderly, savagely, and now they faced each other across a table at Alice's restaurant on the old Malibu Pier.

"You have a little bruise on your neck," Strip said.

"I'm not surprised. I'm sure it's not the only one."

"You're beautiful, you know that? You could be my mother, you're old enough, and you're beautiful. I wish you was my mother, you know that?"

"Do you? But then we couldn't . . . you know."

"Couldn't what?"

"You know."

"Say it."

"No. Not now."

"The way you say it, it's a nice word." He reached across the table and put the back of his hand gently on her breast. "If you was my mother I bet we'd do it anyway. I can feel you."

"Would we? Good. I wouldn't care. I'd do anything with you."

"Why?"

"Because of the way you are."

"Any other reason?"

"Because you make me have no shame at all."

"Anything else? Because you love me?"

117

"Oh, yes. Because I love you."

"Coffee?" It was the voice of the waiter, a college guy in jeans and a shirt, and all three of them burst into laughter as Strip withdrew his hand. Trisha's and Strip's thoughts were as one: high, joyous, immersed in one another. The sea, the pier, the world floated around them and they loved everyone and everything in the world.

"Let's have some cognac with our coffee," Trisha said.

"What ack?"

"Brandy. Two Remy Martins and two espressos."

When the coffee and the cognac came Strip sniffed at them, drew back in mock intoxication at the cognac, and said that the coffee reminded him of the Cookstore shop, where he had tried to get her attention. Had she recognized him?

"Yes," she said.

"But you didn't want to be friendly, huh? Why not?"

"I don't know."

"You were afraid of me, right? You thought I was some punk out to rape you, right?"

"I guess so. If I'd only known."

"Yeah."

"I'd really have been afraid of you."

"Oh, yeah?"

"It's what I told you, I'm a respectable married woman. I don't go around doing it with—boys."

"Right!" He grinned at her over his glass, then sipped at it and grimaced.

"Let it roll around in your mouth," she said, "before you swallow it."

"You really know what you're doing, don't ya?"

They were content then just to look at each other, their feet pressing against each other's.

"What's goin' on in your head?" Strip asked.

"Terrible things."

"Anything else?"

"Yes. I was wondering what you're going to do with your life."

"I been wonderin' about that too. Like twenty-four hours a day."

"You can do anything you want."

"Sure."

"I mean it."

"How come I'm so special?"

"Well, look. I've got incredible taste. Don't you trust me?"

"You gonna make me rich? How about you and me rip off your old man and split to South America! That'll fix him for foolin' around with some bitch, what's her name?"

"Stacy. You're crazy."

"How'd he make all that bread? I bet he invented 'ludes or somethin'."

"Real estate."

"Yeah? The best piece of real estate he ever got was you. I think he's a lousy businessman. I bet he goes bust in a year."

"He won't. Not even if I divorce him. He's got money I don't even know about. He's the cautious type."

"He's a first-class jerk."

"How could he be? I married him."

"You got me there."

Trisha rather liked his jealousy, found it touching, and she felt sorry for him when he squirmed and looked away as the waiter brought the check, which she quickly took. Strip excused himself and disappeared into the men's room. He could not bear to be present when she paid, and Trisha thought how stupid all the vanities and customs imposed on people were. She was a rich woman, he hadn't a cent. Yet the world frowned on a woman giving money to a man. She thought of all the times she had felt uncomfortable being paid for, having checks picked up for her, or how irritating it was, this custom, this imposition of the man always paying. It had occurred to her to give in to custom and to slip Strip some money, so he could pay the check, but she would not, could not surrender to such a stupid farce. A woman was somehow always singing for her supper.

They walked out to the end of the pier, talking of the moon, smelling the air that seemed to them, that night, not just sea air but the freshest air ever, anywhere, in all their lives; and they watched old men and children fishing. They nestled in a corner at the end of the pier, the wind brisk against them, and they kissed, reveling in the warmth and in the smooth, fragrant softness of their faces and bodies in the cool night.

"I gotta do something with myself," Strip said.

"You will."

"No, I mean it. I get scared sometimes. I don't wanna go under. I have this fantasy of

myself ending up in some room somewhere.
I'm about twenty-five or thirty and I'm in this
shitty room that stinks, and there's no one to
call."

"Strip."

"You can't understand. You always had a
roof over your head I bet. I bet your father was
rich too, right?"

"We weren't poor."

"See? I could go under. I really could."

"You won't. You can always call me. Forever.
There'll never be no one to call."

"You mean that?"

"Of course I do. I swear it. But you mustn't
think that way. You've got to think of, you
know, exploiting your talents."

"What talents?"

"Oh. I could name one or two. But I wasn't
thinking of those."

They held each other tightly.

"I'm thinkin'," Strip said, his voice with just
the slightest tremor to it, "if I can get somebody like you to care about me, I got hope, you
know? I mean. Shit. I been hustlin' for so long.
You don't know what goes down. Oh, fuck it.
The trouble with you is you're so nice, you
make me feel like I got a right to feel sorry for
myself. Screw it."

"But Strip . . ."

"But what? The sky's the limit, right? Sure.
Maybe I should go into politics. I could be
governor, right? All I got to do is get together
with a coupla hundred thousand. Go right to
the top. No, wait, I'll go into business. Wildcat
oil. Well, goddamn it, I know I can do some-

thing. Other people done it. I just been goin' at it the wrong way. I been too nice, for one thing. I gotta let loose my killer instinct."

"You don't know what you're talking about."

"No, you don't. Look at you. Who paid for that dinner tonight? You? Or your old man's real estate? And how you think he got his pile together? Being a nice guy?"

She refused to be offended. Instead she drew him to her and said, "Maybe I'm the only one who knows how talented you are. Don't be so modest. I think you're incredible."

"I think I need you."

"You don't need me. You don't need anybody. I love you, that's all."

They clung to each other, looking down at the water spilling against the strong old pylons, while the men and the children went on fishing.

That night was the first time Strip had been in her bedroom. He could not help but feel a sense of triumph mixed with unease as he ascended those stairs, entering the secret top half of the house. They had come back almost like an old married couple, familiar, domestic, content, as the dogs greeted them hysterically. Trisha had fixed strong tea and they had drunk it cuddling the dogs on the couch and talking inanely. Then they had gone up to bed.

For Strip it was like entering forbidden territory. The room was her husband's too, after all, and he had slept with her in that bed. Whatever animosity Strip harbored toward Stu, he felt uneasy at the invasion of another man's territory, and up here Trisha seemed somehow a part of it. However thrilling it was to take

Moment
by Moment™

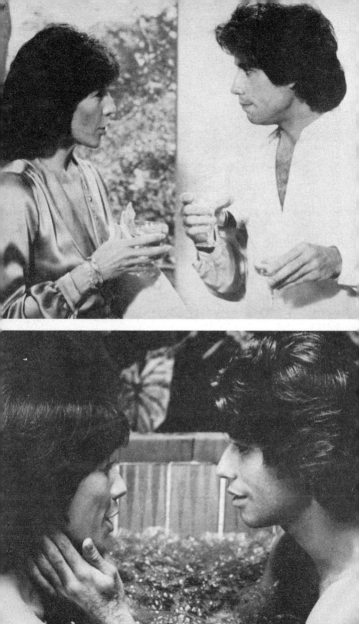

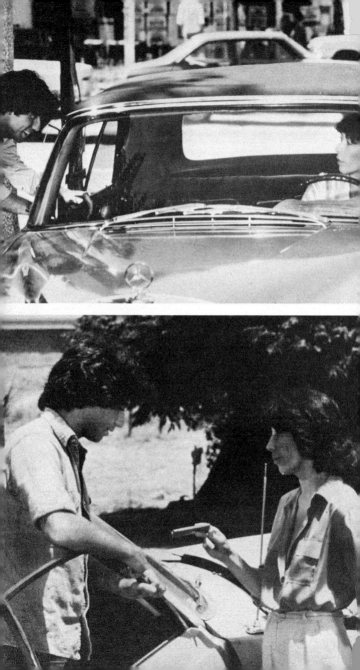

what the social code said belonged to another man, it was also disturbing. Trisha filled the room with a feminine presence. The air was full of perfumes, scented clothes, and he delighted in her undressing, her discarding of the loose Mexican dress she had been wearing. He watched, taking off his own clothes, as she hung the dress on a hanger, placed it in a closet. Even the sound of the hangers being pushed along their wooden bar pleased him, and the sight of her body arched, breasts forward, buttocks pulled in, as she adjusted the clothes, her long, graceful arms extending, gave him sensuous, aesthetic pleasure. If he had ever seen them, he might have thought of certain French paintings of women at their tasks, combing their hair, arranging flowers, but he had not seen them. He could only think: Class. And, almost: Beauty.

They piled into the big bed with its fresh sheets, and again Strip felt himself an invader. Cliché images of angry husbands with guns flashed through his mind. He stared out at the moon through the French doors Trisha had left open. Leaning on one arm, he looked down at her.

"You must be gettin' sick of me sayin' I love you like a broken record."

She reached up for him but, as though it had been put there by some joker, her heavy charm bracelet caught him in the eye. He winced, groaned, and they laughed.

"Did I hurt you?"

"Not really. You oughta take it off, though. Look at that thing. It's dangerous, for chrissakes. Besides, I bet every one of those things has a memory attached to it."

"Does that bother you?"

"A little."

She held it up to him and he struggled with the clasp, muttering about sentiments and memories.

"Those thing change," she said. "I never think of them now. I just like it because it's pretty."

"It must of cost a mint. You'd think for all that they'd make it easier to get off." He finally undid it. "What's this one stand for? The four-leaf clover. Your anniversary?"

"I don't even remember. Come here."

She pulled his head down onto her breasts, running her fingers through his hair.

"Did you notice," she said, "your hair is like mine? Our hair is almost the same length."

"You tryin' to tell me somethin'?"

"Just that I like it. What's the matter?"

"Nothin'. I can't get over this place you have. And all your things."

"Jealous?" He didn't answer. "Are you?"

"No."

"You sure?"

"I just wish I'd given 'em to you. You feel nice. I can hear your heart."

"Are you jealous you don't have them?"

"No. Sort of. I don't know. Maybe I am."

"It's all right. I understand."

She went on stroking his hair. She took strands of her hair and mingled them with his, then took his hand and moved it up to their hair.

"Can you tell whose it is?" she asked.

"No."

"I can't either. I think we're a lot alike."

"Yeah? I think so too."

"We are. We're so much alike. I think that's good."

"Is it?"

"Yes. Feel this. Is that my leg or yours?"

"I don't know. Yours. Ours."

"Ours, yes. And this? Is this yours or mine?"

"Jesus. I don't know."

"Roll over," she said. "On your stomach."

"I don't know if I can."

"Do it."

He rolled over and she climbed onto his back, pressing herself into his buttocks.

Eleven

THE radio, tuned to KLAC at Strip's request, sent country rock and disc-jockey patter into the air. The fog had rolled back early, and by late morning Trisha was sitting on the beach listening to Emmylou Harris and watching Strip build a sandcastle, sculpted, turreted. He went at his work with the intensity of a royal architect, as though he were building for posterity.

"Think I'd make a good disc jockey?" he called. "This is SonnySunsetStrip Harrison sending you the *Really big ones* and be *Ready* out there 'cause Call a *Dummy* Time is *coming right up* . . ."

"You can do anything you want. It looks like you could build castles if you wanted to."

"Hey! Get me a job with your old man. Tell him you'll take him back on a part-time basis if he lets me build his condos. How about it?"

"Think of something a little more subtle."

"I could be a vet."

"You could."

" 'Cept I hate needles."

"You get your nurse to handle that."

"Yeah. Listen, I gotta do somethin'. You know there's one thing I'm getting so's I can't stand any more. Just getting by, you know. Day by day. Moment by moment."

"That's what we're all doing," Trisha said, "if

129

it makes you feel any better. That's what I'm doing."

"Yeah, but you got a bankroll. That makes a hell of a difference. I'll trade moments with you any day." He stood back to appraise his work. "Not bad."

"It's fantastic."

"Yeah, and as soon as the tide comes in: Smash."

"That's the point of a sandcastle, silly. That's the whole point."

"You don't say."

Trisha went inside and returned with an SX-70 Polaroid. Strip watched her as she considered several angles, then got down on one knee and snapped. They waited as the magical process began, the picture rolling out and the image gradually emerging. It was a great shot of the masterpiece with Strip in the background, grinning and proud. Trisha posed Strip with the dogs and took another picture: Another winner, but as they were enjoying it Corky and Scamp took off and tore through the sandcastle, toppling most of it before they could be stopped.

"Look at that!" Strip said. "All my work—ruined! I'll kill myself."

"Pretend that hundreds of years have passed," Trisha said. "The barbarians have invaded. Every dog must have its day."

"You ain't kidding. Okay, now I'll take one of you."

"Not the way I look. Come on, I want you to go shopping for me."

But Strip took the camera and got Trisha to

turn toward him as she was about to climb the steps. He snapped.

"Now what do I do?"

"Just wait. I wish you'd let me brush my hair."

The picture was perfect, flattering to Trisha, with a corner of the house framed nicely.

"I have to admit," she said, "that's a terrific picture."

"You like the way you look? You should."

"I don't mean just that. See the way you got the house in there? And you made it candid and alive."

"So now I'm a great photographer. Boy, another morning like this and I'll be a millionaire."

Trisha held out an arm to him and drew him to her.

"The trouble with you," she said to him softly, kissing him on his hair, "is that nobody's ever encouraged you. Don't you see? You do everything well. You're just one of those people."

"You should of seen my marks in school."

"That doesn't matter. I'm not just talking. You do everything well."

He was too embarrassed to reply. From time to time he had dared hold the same opinion of himself, but nobody else ever had. He had been told he was lazy and worthless and dumb since he could remember. He wanted to believe Trisha. He felt he almost could, but he was flustered and grateful and proud all at once. This goddamned woman, he thought. How'd I get so lucky?

Trisha was in the bedroom changing when Maria, her maid, telephoned to say she would be coming down to the beach to help out. Trisha managed to discourage her with a lot of talk about wanting to be alone and being able to manage all right for the time being. Then she diverted the conversation with plans for Tim's return, making sure his room was in order, though it could hardly be anything else since he hadn't been in it for six months.

Trisha thought about Tim, after Maria had hung up. He was everything that Strip was not, a good student, a kid who had known what he was going to be, a lawyer, since he had been a freshman in high school. Tim was already debating the merits of various law schools with his father. He was a good boy, and Trisha liked to think that she and Stu must have done something right, since their friends were always complaining about ungrateful children, taking drugs and getting into trouble with the police in spite of having all the advantages. Trisha loved Tim. But now, reluctant as she was to admit it, she recognized that he lacked something, a spark, an energy, a furious, intense involvement with life that Strip had. There was something a little cold about Tim. There was nothing cold about Strip. Had Tim been given too much? Strip would be at the market now, shopping with such an appealing eagerness, examining every vegetable, every piece of fruit, seeking perfection as though his life depended on it, cherishing the moment as though the world might come to an end in a minute. With Tim, as with Stu, it was always the future, the future: planning, scheming, being cautious, doing the right thing, making sure you had the right cards before you played them. People like that always came out on top, it seemed. And they made the best husbands, didn't they? Maybe Stu was running around now because he needed to do something reckless for a change. Maybe the men who turned into adolescents in middle age were the ones who had never really had an adolescence, who had never lived freely, who had spent all their lives scheming and planning, oblivious to the present. All those new books that were coming out about the stages and passages of life: Did it really have to be that predictable? Wasn't it all an after-the-fact analysis of the stupid patterns that people impose on themselves, the patterns that come with doing what is expected of you? What of herself? Wasn't this affair rather predictable: What a middle-aged, dutiful housewife does when time seems suddenly about to run out? The thought depressed her.

A noise from downstairs broke her reverie. It was Naomi, calling out in her ebullient way. Strip must have left the door unlocked. He wasn't used to the burden of possessions.

"I'm up here," Trisha shouted.

"You left the door unlocked," Naomi said, coming up the stairs. "That's not like you."

"I forgot."

Naomi came into the room, hugged Trisha, and collapsed on the bed.

"I see you're alive and well. I've been calling and calling."

"I haven't been answering the phone. You

133

know, a little peace and quiet. Very welcome, sometimes."

"My dear, that's all very well, but you needn't become a hermit. What if you'd been dead?"

"That would just about settle it, wouldn't it?"

"You know what I mean. Somebody could break in here and slash your throat. It happens all the time. I was worried. And so was Stu. He wanted to come out. He was afraid to upset you."

"Good."

"Aren't you being a bit stubborn?"

"Honestly, I wish you'd stop worrying about me. Both of you. I'm sorry you had to drive all the way out . . ."

"I had to come out anyway. They've almost finished the new room on our house. Oh, God! I've made a terrible mistake. Remember I decided on cedar instead of redwood?"

"Yes."

"A disaster! The whole thing looks like an enormous closet! It's too late now. We'll have to use it to put people away for the winter. Maybe we can put Stu in there."

Trisha was barely listening. She spotted Strip's cut-offs draped across a chair. Were they definitely male? Not really, but Naomi would know they weren't Trisha's.

"Why don't we go down?" Trisha said. "Let's have a drink." Naomi was staring at the cutoffs and Trisha started out the door.

"I'd adore a Bloody Mary," Naomi said, settling herself in at the breakfast table, changing chairs to stay out of the sun.

"Gin or vodka?"

"Both!"

Trisha giggled, relaxing, and told Naomi she had missed her. In truth she hadn't thought about Naomi at all, but she didn't wish to be unkind. Naomi had been her closest friend for years. It was funny how a close friend could seem so important and then so irrelevant. Trisha put the drinks on the table.

"Fix one for yourself," Naomi said. "Live it up." They laughed and hugged and kissed each other, and Trisha said that there was one thing about Naomi, she could always be counted on for a laugh, and after all, what was more important than that? I could think of a couple of things, Trisha said to herself even as she spoke.

"Before I forget," Naomi said, "Peg made me promise to beg you to come see her opening. She's been trying to reach you. Like the rest of us. Anyway, we both agree it would be good and brave and very useful for you to show your face. Give everybody a chance to see you're still in one piece and shut them up. You know how it is. A woman's alone for five minutes and everyone expects total disintegration.

"You are all right, aren't you? You look well."

"I'm doing very well."

"I was going to say. You look positively vibrant. What's your secret? All this fresh air, I suppose. Isn't it marvelous?"

"It is. Wonderful."

"Sometimes I think we're fools not to just move to the beach. But then everything's so far, don't you find?"

"I haven't wanted to go out much."

"Of course. Now, what about the gallery? Will you go to Peg's opening or not? Of course you will."

"I don't know," Trisha said. "It depends on how I feel, I rather doubt it, to tell you the truth. It doesn't sound too thrilling."

"I can't say I'm looking forward to it myself that much, but guess what her theme is? Go on, guess."

"I can't imagine."

Naomi laid out the theme of the gallery opening. It was to be a photography show. Some young genius had taken hundreds of photographs of feet.

"Human feet?" Trisha asked.

"I didn't think to ask. Maybe pig's feet, for all I know. The show is called Footography. Isn't that cute?"

"You must be kidding."

"I didn't like it either. Peg's ideas always seem to fall a wee bit short, to put it kindly. Still, you never can tell what people go for. Look at that absolute creep who's cleaning up on, I don't know, whatever it is. Anyway, Peg got the idea because the gallery's next to a shoe store. There's genius for you!"

"She'll do well. She always does. I admire her energy. What's the point of having any sort of idea if you don't do anything with it?"

"Oh, she'll make a fortune, like most people with second-rate ideas."

"I have to admire her," Trisha said. "She's completely self-sufficient."

"So is a caterpillar. Why is that such a virtue?

I admit it. I'm completely unself-sufficient. I wouldn't want it any other way. And one of the things I love about you is that you never say anything bad about anybody, no matter what you think, and so I know you'll stand up for me when I make an ass of myself, which is every two minutes. So I'll tell Peg you're coming."

"Naomi—please. I don't want to make up my mind yet."

Suddenly Strip was through the front door and into the kitchen, carrying two heavy grocery sacks, flashing Trisha a big smile. She felt herself panic and before she could think she heard herself say:

"Just put them in there, thank you very much," and she was up digging in her purse. She held out a dollar to Strip.

He looked at the money, at her, at Naomi. He started to laugh, then realized she was serious. It seemed an hour of silence passed. The color drained from his face, his mouth went slack. Quickly he turned and hurried out, slamming the front door.

Trisha looked at the money in her hand and heard a ringing in her ears. "Naomi," she said, because there was no reason not to say something now, "I've just done something terrible."

"I had that impression." Trisha slumped down, tears welling in her eyes. "Trisha. What is it? What have you been up to?"

She did not respond. She sat lifeless for a minute, holding back emotion, trying to decide what to do. Then she remembered the address book that had brought them back together before, and she fetched it from beside the telephone.

"I've got to go into town," Trisha said.

"You want to find him, don't you? Where does he live?"

"Western Avenue."

"Western Avenue? You sure pick 'em. I'll go with you. You wouldn't want to go there by yourself. You can tell me all about it in the car."

"All right," Trisha said, too shaken to object, loathing herself for what she had done.

Twelve

"I can't believe it," Naomi said as they turned onto Sunset. "And slow down, for God's sake. I've never seen you drive like this. What's going on with you?"

"I don't know," Trisha said. She was scarcely listening, intent only on getting to Strip's neighborhood as quickly as possible.

"Of all my friends," Naomi said, "you're the one I thought I could trust never to make a fool of herself." Trisha said nothing. "What's going on? Everyone's gone mad. Ann's run off with her hairdresser, and everyone *knows* he's in love with Frank. Gail is off disco-dancing every night with her decorator, and God knows he's pretty suspect. Peg is a coke fiend. I'm beginning to feel awfully old-fashioned. Apparently, you're just not in it at all these days if you're not running around. But you! How old did you say he is? My God, I certainly did think he was the delivery boy." Trisha gave her a quick, cold look. "Don't get me wrong! I'm not judging. It's to your credit, really, I guess. I'm a little new to these things."

"Don't make such a big deal out of it," Trisha said.

They drove in silence for a while. Trisha switched on the radio, ran through all the stations, and switched it off.

141

"We lead very enclosed lives, you know," Trisha said.

"You've certainly changed that."

"No, I haven't. I don't really know that much about him. I don't think I understand him. I don't think I could. I've been isolated too long."

"What's to understand? You sure he isn't out for your money?"

"Of course I thought that. I was wrong. Strip is a complete romantic. Incurable."

"Or a great con artist."

"No. He says I'm *alluring*. Or he did. Now he says he loves me."

"Sure, he does. A real puppy dog."

"In a way, yes."

Trisha tried to explain what had been passing between herself and Strip, without wanting to be disloyal or to make him seem ridiculous, but she could not really get through. Naomi was so anxious to find some way of putting the whole thing into an acceptable perspective, some way of making it an aberration or a joke or both, that the idea it might be tender, alive, exciting, and, yes, very much worth having was beyond her.

"Look at it this way," Trisha said. "Supposing it's just plain lust. What's wrong with that? If it's all right for men, why not women?"

"Why not?" Naomi said, obviously convinced.

By the time they reached the La Paula, Trisha had begun to feel Naomi had come along less for company and less as protection against random psychopaths than as a chaperone, in case they did actually find Strip. She resented this a little, yet she knew Naomi meant well. Naomi was dependent on the structured world that was

encompassed by Bel-Air, Beverly Hills, and
Malibu. If you ventured outside, it was perhaps to the Music Center or to certain areas of
New York City and Europe. You might go to a
ball game at Dodger Stadium, but even there
you sat in certain seats, gravitated toward certain concession stands: You could sit in a crowd
with fifty thousand people from all parts of the
city, rednecks, Mexicans, blacks, and be aware
of them only as images and voices, never actually encountering them. And everywhere you
went in the city you were enclosed in your car.
Strip had come into Trisha's life like a visitor
from another planet. For years she had scarcely
spoken to anyone outside her circle or beneath
her economic class. Now she was *sleeping* with
one of *them*. The idea was far more shocking
than the reality. The reality wasn't shocking at
all. It was pleasant.

They had reached the 1600 block of Western.
They searched for numbers and scanned the
signs: Brankrupt Discount Store; Flama Latina
(Matlos Maribel Presenting Latin Review);
Piece o' Pizza (Had a Piece Lately?); Time
Motel ($8 Siesta, $10 Single, $12 Double);
House of Hermetics; Hollywood Roxy Hotel.

"This must be it," Naomi said. "It's got the
right ambience. You must be nuts."

Trisha pulled over and parked. She got out,
Naomi following reluctantly, pausing with the
door half open as a bent old man crept along
the sidewalk. They had parked in front of
Jonie's Adult Books/Movie Arcade/International
Love Boutique. Naomi found herself drawn to
the window, peering in. An array of dildoes, in-

flatable women, fur-lined manacles: one rubber object, vaguely resembling a hot water bottle, puzzled her, and she looked around for Trisha, who was searching out numbers on doorways. "Trisha! Come look at this!"

They stared together at the object.

"What the hell is that?" Naomi said.

"This isn't the place."

"I wouldn't be surprised if it were. Too bad it isn't. What is that?"

"What do you think?"

"It's not a dildo."

"Try again."

"You're kidding. Ooogh! Disgusting!" But she gave a good, strong laugh. Trisha hurried her along.

They found the La Paula, and, to Naomi's horror, Trisha pushed in the door and went right in, past the lobby, which consisted of one filthy couch with the stuffing pouring out of it, and up the foul-smelling stairs. Naomi wanted to tell Trisha to stop but was trying to breathe through her mouth and couldn't get the words out. She wondered whether Trisha had actually come here with that kid, and she conjured up hideous deviations perpetrated amid animal filth.

Trisha knocked insistently on Strip's door, then paused. When she knocked again a man appeared from down the hall.

"Whadda yiz want?" he called, moving toward them. He was a big, shapeless man in an undershirt, with a purple face and a nose on it the size of a fist.

144

"Strip Harrison," Trisha said. "We're looking for him."

"He don't live here no more," the man said, scrutinizing them. "He owe you money? The son of a bitch owes me the week's rent. Cleaning deposit. The son of a bitch owes me twenty bucks. Thirty. Where can I find that son of a bitch?"

"He didn't leave a forwarding address?" Trisha asked.

The man broke into a spasm of laughing and coughing, bending over, losing his breath. Trisha and Naomi backed off and raced down the stairs.

"Did you see that?" Naomi said when they were out in the street. "Nauseating."

Trisha was flipping through Strip's address book. Naomi suggested that they go get a cup of coffee.

"I feel a little weak," she said.

At the Gold Cup Coffee Shop on Hollywood Boulevard they sat, watching the tourists and the addicts and the whores go by.

"Don't you think," Naomi said, "that where a person lives, I mean the type of people he hangs around, says something about him? I mean, even being poor, you don't have to live around here, do you? There must be inexpensive places all over. You take those apartments down around south Robertson. I bet they don't go for more than two hundred dollars a month. Unfurnished, of course."

"You don't know what it is to have nothing," Trisha said. "I don't either. At least not till recently."

Naomi was finally moved by Trisha's serious-
ness. Clearly she wanted to find Strip, clearly
she cared about him, but she was not making a
fool of herself over him at all. She seemed concerned, agitated, yet in control of herself, as
though she understood precisely what she was
doing. She had insulted the boy and wanted to
make things right with him, but it was more as
though she had wronged a friend than that she
was desperate over some half-perverted affair.

"You really do care for him?" Naomi asked.

"I don't know," Trisha said. "None of the
clichés apply, somehow. He keeps wanting me
to say I love him, for instance. I'll say it, I do
do feel some sort of love for him, but I couldn't
tell you what it all means. Why does it have to
mean anything? Why do we have to define
everything? Maybe it's just screwing, maybe it
isn't, I don't know. I know he's very sweet. He's
also rather astonishingly good-looking."

"I noticed that."

"Well? If you talked to him for five minutes
you'd see other things too."

"I just can't imagine myself—" Naomi hesitated. "But then, I'm not you. You know, for
someone who's supposed to have been hurt by
her husband, you're doing incredibly well. As a
matter of fact, you've never looked better. Poor
Stu! He'd die if he knew!"

Trisha decided that they should try a few of
the other addresses in the book, at least the
ones in the immediate neighborhood. Strip
might have been in touch. It was evening now,
too early for the crowds, but the lights were
coming on, the neon of movie theaters, cheap

restaurants. At a disco they inquired after Strip. The manager, a black man wearing a dashiki, knew him and seemed concerned when they told him of Strip's disappearance. He took Trisha's phone number and promised to call if Strip turned up. Naomi, when they left, told Trisha that it had been insane of her to give out her number like that; she was inviting disaster.

"Naomi," Trisha said, getting a little exasperated with her friend, "every time I think you understand, you don't. Couldn't you tell that man was really worried about Strip?"

"Well, I know. But he's—"

"Don't say it."

They tried another disco. Nothing. At an apartment on Wilcox a stunning girl opened the door. She had long, straight blonde hair and green eyes, and her voice in greeting was warm, melodic. When she heard about Strip's vanishing her face clouded over and she shook her head. No, she had not seen him, not for weeks.

"I noticed you didn't give her your number," Naomi said. They were back in the car.

"I was afraid you'd notice that," Trisha said, and they had a good laugh, breaking built-up tensions of the day. "Oh, Naomi. You're a good friend. After all."

"Whoever said I wasn't? You just have to give me a little time to adjust. I never thought of you as a woman of intrigue. From now on I suppose you'll be wanting me to make excuses for you, so you can keep your clandestine appointments with people from the underworld. Don't worry, I'm loyal."

"Are you? I wonder what you really think."

Naomi let Trisha drive on in silence a while. Then she said, "I'm thinking what a bore shopping at Bullock's is going to be from now on!"

At the beach house Naomi offered to spend the night, but Trisha said she'd rather be alone.

"Besides," Naomi said, "he might come back. God knows if he caught sight of me he'd run away again. Good luck, angel. You know something? I admire you. I really do."

"There's nothing to admire," Trisha said. "Believe me."

"Well, I think you have guts."

"It's not guts, Naomi. It's just nice. Or was. Good night."

He came back near midnight. Trisha had sat reading and watching television simultaneously, doing neither really, thinking about him and feeling progressively worse. She was nagged by guilt at having acted so insensitively. She had relied on her instincts and they had turned out to be cowardice and snobbery. Offering him money had been the worst. She despised herself for that and wondered about all her motives toward him. How real was the tenderness she thought she had felt toward him when in two seconds she could treat him like a servant?

But when he knocked and announced himself as the delivery boy, she threw open the door and embraced him as a prodigal son, heaping apologies and kisses on him. The dogs leaped against them, almost knocking them down in the doorway. Strip tried to be aloof, saying nothing and examining Corky's bandaged leg with a critical eye, complaining that the dressing should have been changed, muttering that he had come back for his address book. Again.

"I looked all over for you. Naomi and I—"

"Your friend who was here? She's no friend of mine."

"Strip." She held him and pulled him into the house. "Forgive me."

"Where's my book?"

"Upstairs. In my bedroom."

"Oh. In your bedroom. Well, why don't you get it?"

"Why don't we get it together?" She could tell that his coldness was only an act, and she countered it with: "I want to be in bed with you. Now."

"I'll go get the book," he said.

But upstairs, when Trisha lay back on the bed and held out her arms to him, he came down to her, and they held each other in silence. He was still trying to hold back, but she felt so warm, her strength a refuge for him, her good smells exciting him.

"I don't like what you did today," he said.

"I know. It was rotten."

"Bein' ashamed of me. Made me feel like a nothing."

"You've got to forgive me. I just panicked."

"What're you afraid of?"

"I'm not afraid anymore. I swear I'm not. I'll tell the world. I'll walk naked with you down Wilshire Boulevard."

"I like that."

Trisha tried to explain herself. She cast the worst light on it, saying she had lacked the courage of her feelings, that she had worried about gossip, about looking like a fool in front of her friends. But after all, there was something to be said for her, wasn't there? She couldn't help being self-conscious about being so much older than he: It was easy to say it didn't matter, but obviously it did. It never bothered her when she was with him, but she wasn't entirely immune to what she knew would be the critical view of the world. People could be cruel, he knew that, surely.

"If I don't care how old you are," Strip said, "why do you?"

"I don't. You make me not care."

"You must be really hooked on me."

"I am."

"And you'll never be ashamed again?"

"Never. I want to be in public with you. I want everyone to know. Will you go to a party with me?"

"What kind of a party?"

"An art opening."

"A what? Forget it."

"Come on. Ashamed of me?"

He kissed her and asked her what she would do if he broke her heart, and she said he already had.

"We're even then," he said.

She wanted to know where he had been all day. He said he had just driven around. He had wanted to come back, but his pride kept him away. She told him she had been to his apartment and had a charming conversation with his ex-landlord, who seemed such a decent, reasonable sort of fellow, she couldn't understand why he would ever want to leave a place like that, with all the amenities, so cheerful.

"Cut it out."

"You like it here better?"

"Well, it's not home. But there are some advantages."

"Like this?" She took his hand and put it between her legs. "What's the matter? Do I shock you?"

"A little. No."

"How about this? Does this shock you?"

"Christ."

"I think you're a prude," she said.

"Me? You're kidding."

"No. See? When I do that you're shocked. It's all right. You're just a baby, aren't you?"

"Oh, yeah?"

"Sure. You're just a baby. I have to show you how to act. What to do. Like this." She undid his pants and kissed him.

"Take that back," he said, "about my being a baby."

"No." She raised her head. "You are a baby. But you're growing up. See? I can help you grow up."

"Say it."

"Say what? Okay, okay, I love you."

"I love you too. You're not just sayin' it so—"

"I do love you. Show me you love me. Show me."

Thirteen

SHE took him to Bonwit's and bought him a peach-colored silk shirt. It had taken a lot of arguing to get him to go, but she had found ways of talking him into it, thrilling ways. She had entered a phase with him that was new to her, and she reveled in it. Trisha was not beautiful in any standard way. She had considered herself attractive, once the doubts of adolescence had faded, yet not quite ravishing, her striking, long bones and dark hair compensating perhaps for the lack of anything that could be called voluptuous. But now, with Strip, she felt possessed of tremendous sexual power. That he responded to her the way he did was a part of it, but it seemed, this power, to enter into everything she did, every act, every gesture: to make everything come easily and naturally, harmoniously. In bed or out she felt as natural and as ceaselessly energetic as the sea, and like the sea she enveloped him, surrounded him, moved him this way and that.

When he emerged from the dressing room in the clothes she was buying, she felt the prideful thrill usually enjoyed only by men, when they see a pretty girl parade for them in a new dress, showing off in a store for them, in front of people: a sexual, thrilling pride that connects lovers and a wallet. And so powerful were her feelings that they overcame Strip's embarrassment and gave him pleasure. He was embarrassed. He did have difficulty accepting what she insisted on giving him. But he could not resist her and, giving in, he luxuriated in the surrender.

She took him to lunch in his new clothes at the Cafe Swiss on Rodeo Drive, where they ate outside on the patio, surrounded by people refreshing themselves from the exhaustion that spending lots of money can bring, talking fashion, making deals, complaining about alimony and cleaning women.

"I'm not sure I belong here," Strip said.

"Of course you do. You're the best-looking person here. You make the rest of them look dead."

"I'm the only one here who doesn't have any money."

"In the first place, that's not true. Half of these people are in debt up to their ears, you know that. And besides, what difference does it make? You have me. I have money. So you have money too."

"Do I really have you?"

"Any time. Now."

Next to them a bald man wearing a silk suit and an open-necked shirt was talking loudly about condominiums. The market was down but a turn-around was coming. These were high-class places, the location was high-class, if he just hung on for six more months he would have a profit of thirty-five percent. With the gimmick he would work on taxes, it would be even better than that. It would be one of the best deals he had ever made.

"Arnie," he said to his companion, a younger man impeccably dressed in fawn-colored linen, "you shoulda come in with me."

"I'll believe it when I see it," Arnie said. "I think you're overbuilt."

"I'm with Arnie," Strip said to Trisha.

"See what you're missing?" Trisha said. "You could be a big businessman and sit around talking like that all day."

"Like your husband?"

"Well, yes. Like my husband."

"And what'd you be doing?"

"I'd be off with—someone. I'd be off with someone very young and incredibly handsome. I'd be sitting in a nice restaurant drinking champagne and staring at him, rubbing his leg with my foot, thinking about everything I'm going to do with him. To him."

"And what about me? Say I'm your husband."

"Too bad for you. You had your chance."

They went to see *The Turning Point* that afternoon and later, in the car, driving to they weren't sure where, Strip asked Trisha if she had ever wanted to go to work. She told him that she had done well in college, had been an English major, and had been accepted by graduate schools. She had considered being a college teacher or doing something connected with books, but Stu had come along, and Tim, and somehow having all that money had made working seem pointless. At least it had taken away whatever incentive she might have had. Recently she had begun to think she had made a mistake, but she wasn't going to be one of

those women who go back to school in middle age. What would she do if she did get an advanced degree? Start out teaching someplace in a junior position, if she could get a job at all? No. Some things were right for you when you were a certain age, and then it was too late. But yes, she had begun to regret not having some sort of career. She had to resent being dependent on Stu, especially now, and if they did split up permanently, she didn't like the idea of living off his money for the rest of her life. Maybe she would go to work then, someplace. She had friends who were rich and who worked anyway, some of them at fashionable stores, for low salaries. There was something distasteful about that. Volunteer work didn't appeal to her either. She didn't mix with the fund raisers, the charity crowd. She was pretty much of a loner, maybe too much so. Maybe she had become a bore to Stu. Strip wouldn't hear of that. He steered her back to how she felt about being dependent on her husband.

"How come you say I shouldn't mind taking your money if you mind taking his?"

She couldn't answer that one. "I don't know," she said finally. "Look at it this way. We're both taking his money, okay? We're both crooks and spongers. Is that better?"

"Sort of," he said.

"We deserve it, don't we? I think we do."

"If you say so," he said. "By the way, how about I drive?"

She pulled over and Strip came around and slid behind the wheel. He drove south and turned onto the Santa Monica Freeway, heading east, away from the beach. Trisha asked him where he was going but he said he wanted to surprise her. When he got onto the San Bernardino Freeway she wondered aloud whether he was taking her to see his parents.

"I'm impressed," she said. "It's what every well-brought-up young man should do. 'Hi, Mom. Hi, Dad. I'd like to introduce you to Mrs. Rawlings. Mrs. Rawlings is my mistress. We make love all day and all night.'"

"No. I'm takin' you to a place I like, that's all. If I gotta go to that goddamned art show with you, you can come someplace with me."

Trisha was more than happy to go along, though she hadn't a clue to what he had in mind. Some friends of his? That might be awkward. She imagined herself sitting in some run-down house with a bunch of teenagers, passing joints and drinking cheap wine, talking about astrology, feeling like everyone's mother. That would drive her out of her mind. But she had to let Strip take her where he wanted, for once. After all, she had been managing their brief life together completely.

"You taking me to an orgy?" she asked.

"No. That where you want to go?"

"No. I don't think I could do that. Stu had some ideas along that line a couple of years ago. I made it plain it wasn't for me."

"I'm glad to hear that."

"Still, it might be different, with you."

"How?"

"I don't know. With you, I might get excited enough, I might do almost anything."

They drove past Pomona and got off the freeway at Central Avenue, in Upland.

"Where are you taking me?"

"You'll see."

"I didn't think there was anything out here but oranges. No, wait. There was a place out here. A Mexican restaurant in the hills where they used to put on plays and Mexican dancing. Padua Hills. Is that where we're going?"

"No, it ain't. Does that sound like me?"

It was dark now. They passed a shopping center, an orange grove, and then Strip pulled into a crowded parking lot next to a small building with a sign saying Uncle Ned's.

"What is this, a bar?"

"You'll see."

"I love it. I haven't been to a dive in years. Not since college."

"It's not really a dive. Though I notice we got the only Mercedes." The parking lot was full of pick-ups, old Chevies.

"I'm overdressed," Trisha said. "But so are you. Besides, nobody's going to see my Pucci underwear."

"Yeah. Let's leave your Pucci outa this."

Inside, a drummer, a blind man with a guitar, and a young singer, her black hair piled up into a huge hive, were doing their best with "Silver Threads and Golden Needles." Couples crowded the tiny dance floor, clinging together as though it were 1948. Strip led Trisha to a small, dark booth in a corner, where they could watch the band and the dancers. It was impossible to talk above the noise, so they held hands, glancing at each other and smiling, and when a waitress came over wearing hotpants and a T-shirt saying "Drinkers Make Better Lovers," Strip shouted at her, "Draw two! Oh, I forgot. The lady don't like beer."

"I'll have one," Trisha said.

She studied the crowd. They were mostly middle-aged and over, but there were younger couples too, and several who looked like college kids. The men favored short hair and had beer bellies, the women wore everything from pantsuits to sweaters and skirts. They all seemed to be having a hell of a good time.

When the band took a break, Trisha asked Strip who these people were.

"Americans," he said.

"No, seriously."

"I am serious. They're just ordinary working people, like me."

"You're not like them."

"Yes, I am. Except maybe I went to L.A. and I'm hustlin' and I got halfway in with a buncha crooks and I'm livin' in some rich woman's house. And I kinda lost touch with them. They're like my parents."

"You still love your parents, don't you?"

"Sure. Don't you?"

"Would you call these people rednecks?"

"If you want to call 'em rednecks, just let me know ahead of time. I told you. They're just Americans. God-fearin', gun-totin', beer-drinkin,' fun-loving' Americans."

"The kind that built this country up."

"You got it."

She could tell that he wasn't really kidding, though he knew that there was already a gap

between him and his people and that it was
widening every day. Someday it would be un-
bridgeable. Maybe she was helping him widen
it, maybe that's what she was for in his life.
She had scarcely thought at all of anything she
might be doing for him, so caught up had she
been in what he was doing for her.

"You like being different from these people,
don't you, Strip?"

"Not really. I like 'em. Why'd you think I
brought you here? Come on. The band's back.
Let's dance."

Trisha felt extremely self-conscious on the
floor at first, but then she realized that no one
was paying any attention to them and she relaxed, happy to be guided by him. She knew
that he hung around discos in Hollywood but
he seemed to take easily to this sort of dancing,
the kind she remembered from high school,
cheek-to-cheek or with little spin-outs and
twirls. The band ran through "That Silver-
Haired Daddy of Mine" and "Room Full of
Roses," which everyone cheered for. Then it
was "Release Me." They held each other, hardly
dancing at all, and listened to the sad lyrics
that told of lovers parting. Trisha felt like crying. And she felt ridiculous. Here she was in
this dump listening to this dumb, corny music,
and she felt like crying.

She felt less ridiculous when she saw tears
in Strip's eyes.

"Come on," she said. "Let's sit down."

It was very hot. Trisha couldn't tell the sweat
from the tears on her face. She pressed the
cool beer glass to her cheek and patted herself

with the damp paper napkin, looking at Strip, who was blowing his nose as the song ended. Somehow it all seemed suddenly funny, and they laughed together.

"Look at us," Trisha said. "We're just a couple of sentimentalists."

"Yeah. Crybabies."

"I like this place," she said. "I really do. Thank you for bringing me here."

"I knew you'd like it. It's real. So are you."

Fourteen

THEY were getting ready for the art opening, and Strip was making it obvious that he did not want to go.

"That's not fair," Trisha said, brushing her hair at her dressing table. "How do you know you won't enjoy it as much as I did Uncle Ned's?"

"Wanna make a bet?"

"Well, if you've already made up your mind . . ."

"Who'll be there?"

Trisha said she didn't know—some of her friends and other people she wouldn't know, friends of the artist, potential buyers. These things weren't all that terrifying. They could be boring, and if it was, they'd simply leave. She thought it was important that they didn't hide from people. They couldn't isolate themselves from everyone.

"I could live alone with you and not see anybody," Strip said. "I could stay in this house forever and just watch you brush your hair."

"Come here," she said. "I'll brush yours."

He submitted, a little petulantly, to the strokes, softening under them and enjoying her closeness, her perfume. He knew he hadn't a chance of talking her out of going, yet he couldn't bring himself quite to be resigned to it. He couldn't quell a certain resentment he felt. I'm just her new dog, he said to himself. She wants to show me off. She's grooming me now for the big dog show. Figures I'll get first in class. Low class. She's so used to buying things, she thinks she can buy me like a car or a new dress. Well, can't she? Here I am all dressed up in what she's bought, a dressed-up freak ready to go on show.

The great disadvantage in not having money, Strip had already learned in his short life, was not in going hungry, not even in the anxiety about tomorrow or next week, though he knew that, if he had a family, that anxiety would be paramount, would eat into him day after day and wear him down, as it had his father and his mother. No, the great disadvantage for him was the inferior position it gave him in relation to people who did have money. He had no leverage, no power except his own personality; he had no place to go, so that if he decided to leave a scene it meant returning to a depressing room or running to someone else, being dependent on someone else, currying favor with someone by means of cheerfulness or sex or some wild, crazy scheme that might convince someone to bank on him for a week or a month. That was the curse of being poor in his life and in the world as he knew it. Maybe in some other country they did things differently. Occasionally he caught himself dreaming of an island paradise where the tribe took care of its own; from time to time he thought of becoming a minister or a priest just to be able to count on a decent place to stay and a job that gave him a role to play every day of his life. But he knew there

was no such island for him and that he was
hardly cut out to join the clergy for any reason.
The trouble was, he had a lot of ambition: He
wasn't willing to settle for the steady job with
the pension plan, the sort of security everyone
else seemed to be after, or almost everybody.
Perhaps he wanted more out of life than life
would ever be willing to give him, more out of
life than he would be able to squeeze, wrest, or
choke from it. Yet Trisha seemed to see something in him, a spark, a talent, a potential,
something. Or was she only flattering him to get
what she wanted? Did she have any conception,
really, of what someone in his position faced?
She had reacted exactly as he had hoped to
Uncle Ned's, but how strange it was, her ignorance of those ordinary people. They might
as well have come from Mars, yet there were
more people like them, he knew, than any
others. Maybe he knew more about life than
she did. That was an uncomfortable thought.
It meant that none of her praise and what he
hoped was her love meant a damned thing.
What a joke, if it turned out that this fine
woman he was depending on really had nothing
to give him.

"How do I look?" she asked.

"Beautiful," he said, meaning it. She wore a
steel blue dress of some silky material that
clung to her, her long, graceful arms bare. Out
of deference to him, he noticed, she wore no
jewelry, and this touched him and made him
feel foolish at the same time.

"Wear a bracelet or anything you want," he
said. "I don't mind."

"I'd rather go naked. With you. And look: My dress is the same color as your shirt. We're twins."

"Are we?" he asked. She had made him soften again. He felt stupid about all the negative thoughts he had been having. How could he resist her? How could he question her motives? Just go along, he told himself. She means you no harm. She wants to have a good time. What's the harm in her wanting her friends to meet me? She's right.

"I have an idea," she said. "We'll stop for a drink on the way. Someplace elegant. Where shall we go?"

"I don't know," he said. "You choose."

They stopped at the little bar in the Beverly Wilshire Hotel. She thought first of the obvious Polo Lounge, but it seemed a bit much. She had suggested it, had said with slightly satirical enthusiasm that they could go to the Polo Lounge and be sure to see a few movie stars, but Strip demurred. He had already parked the cars of all the movie stars he needed to see for the time being, he said.

The hotel bar was cool and dark. A television set showed the Dodgers and the Reds.

"I haven't been to a game all year," Strip said. "I usually take in a few."

"Stu has season tickets," Trisha said. "I'm not much of a fan myself. Neither is Stu, for that matter. He gives the tickets away most of the time, for business purposes."

"Yeah. That's why people like me can never get good seats and never get to see the series."

Trisha had begun to notice that it was getting increasingly difficult to bring up any subject that didn't put Strip on the defensive. She was racking her brain more and more often to find some neutral ground that they could share. She ordered a vodka and tonic, he a beer.

"I was a pretty good ballplayer," Strip said. "Not major-league caliber though. I used to dream of playing in the big leagues. I guess every kid does. Your son ever play ball?"

"Some. He's on the lacrosse team at school."

"What's that?"

"It's an old Indian game. They play it a lot in the East. They have sticks with nets on them and a ball. It's very rough. I worry about him but I know it's pointless."

"I never heard of it," Strip said. "Soccer's getting big."

Both of them knew that they were straining for conversation. It was the first time this had happened and it made them uncomfortable. Strip sipped his beer, watched Garvey hit a line-drive double, restrained himself from commenting on it, and tried to think of something else to say. I want to bring up something real, he thought. Get us on the beam again.

"How come you never had any more kids?" he asked suddenly.

"We decided against it," she said without hesitation. It was not a subject she liked to think about, but under the circumstances she almost welcomed it. She was as anxious as Strip was for something more than superficial chat. "I had my tubes tied."

"Why'd you do that," he asked. "How come

you didn't want any more? It ain't like you couldn't afford it."

"Strip, I wish you'd stop talking about money. You're getting obsessed."

"I'm sorry."

"I'll tell you what happened. After I had Tim, I got pregnant again. But the baby didn't survive. It lived for nine days and it died. The doctors said there was a good chance the same thing would happen with any other children I'd have. Actually, Tim had been sickly as an infant, too. I didn't want to go through that again. I'd like to have had another child. I sometimes think about it. But I couldn't go through that again. So I had the operation."

"I'm sorry," Strip said.

"You don't have to be sorry about anything."

"I was being insensitive."

He put his hand on hers. They ordered another round and spent a close, peaceful half hour there in the bar. Then it was time to go.

Strip did not like what he saw from the moment he entered the gallery. To him the whole thing smelled phony. He tried to talk himself into accepting it but from the start he was restless and edgy, and he stuck close to Trisha, sensing that if he opened his mouth to anyone else, it would be disaster.

Strip paid little attention to the exhibit itself. Huge blown-up photographs of human feet, some in black and white and others in color, covered the gallery's walls. It was a small La Cienega gallery, just below Santa Monica Boulevard, with white walls and a pale gray carpet, so that the photographs and the clothes

of the guests stood out sharply in the strong
light. The atmosphere was close and hot as
waiters circulated with trays of champagne and
hors d'oeuvres, water chestnuts wrapped in ba-
con and minuscule hot dogs. Some hundred and
fifty people crowded in, all of them tan. Strip
took two glasses from a tray, handed one to
Trisha, downed his in a gulp, and traded his
empty glass for a full one.

"Take it easy," Trisha whispered to him. He
took his second glass in two swallows and
turned to the wall as a man came up and
greeted Trisha. The wall confronted Strip with
an enormous pair of male feet. The toenails
were long and broken with dirt under them,
and the camera appeared to have been focused
on one prominent corn. Strip heard Trisha say
there was someone she wanted him to meet and
felt her hand on his arm. He decided that whoever it was couldn't be worse than what he
was staring at.

"Strip Harrison, I'd like you to meet Ernst
Gottlieb, an old and dear friend."

"Glad to meet you." Strip held out his hand
and received a firm grip and two brisk, formal
shakes from a man who looked to be somewhere in his sixties, corpulent and cheerful behind thick glasses, a wisp of gray hair standing
up from his shining head.

"Delighted. You are friend of Trisha's, Mrs.
Rawling's?"

"Yeah."

"Vondafool. You are shtudent?"

"Not anymore."

"An artist then?"

"I'm just sorta hangin' loose."

"Yes?"

"Strip is interested in photography," Trisha said. "He has a natural talent for it."

"So!" said Mr. Gottlieb. "And what is your opinion?" He gestured around at the exhibit.

"I can't really go for it," Strip said.

"An intelligent young man," Mr. Gottlieb said, smiling at Trisha. And to Strip: "Ve are in complete agreement. Ve haf here a brilliant collection of rubbish!"

"Garbage," Strip said, a little loud.

Mr. Gottlieb moved in on Strip. He asked in confidential tones how Strip would rank the great photographers. Cartier-Bresson, perhaps, was preeminent, but there was the question of sensational subject matter. Strip said nothing, and Mr. Gottlieb went on to the question of whether photography was an art. How did Strip react to Susan Sontag's argument in *On Photography*? Had we become a culture of image-makers, divorced from reality itself?

Trisha rescued him, pulling him away and apologizing to Mr. Gottlieb that there was someone they had to say hello to. She led him to a corner. A tray of champagne passed by and Strip reached for it eagerly.

"Who was that guy?" he asked.

"He's really very nice," she said. "He was only trying to be friendly."

"What does he do? Is he a photographer?"

"No, he's a dealer."

"In Vegas?"

"He's a rare book dealer. He has a shop on Canon. He's really a very sweet person. He's given me a lot of things and sold me a lot, way under the going price. Wait a minute. There's Naomi."

Strip saw Naomi coming toward them and, in the same instant, he spotted Stu on the other side of the room, wearing tight-fitting flared jeans and a body shirt. Beside him was a tall honey-blonde about half his age wearing a crocheted dress.

"Is that Stacy over there, with your husband?" Strip asked.

"Yes," said Trisha.

"She likes to show her tits, doesn't she?" Strip grabbed another glass of champagne.

"I don't like to see you drink like that," Trisha said.

"I gotta do somethin'." The champagne, he noticed, was beginning to get to him. He felt his head swim a little when he moved it and he was starting to sweat. He wanted to take off his jacket. He wanted to go outside and stay outside. He felt trapped. Naomi sailed up.

"How radiant you look," Naomi bubbled to Trisha. And to Strip she said, exuding friendliness, "She's the only one who can still look original in a Halston original!" When Strip did not respond, she went on, looking him up and down, "You are something. No wonder she was so frantic to find you the other day. I wish we'd looked harder! Are you having a good time? No, of course you're not. Aren't these things ghastly? But we have to do them. The way of the world!"

In the silence that followed the three of them looked around the room vacantly, until Naomi, unable to contain herself, leaned toward Trisha and whispered to her in tones that Strip could overhear that it would be an excellent and shrewd idea to take Strip around a bit, show him off, let everybody, including a certain very specific party, get a good look at them together, because it would be worth it, wouldn't it, just to see the look on Stu's face. Strip felt his blood pound.

Trisha tried to edge toward him.

"Please," Naomi pursued her. "It's just what he deserves. And what's more important"— here she cupped her hand over Trisha's retreating ear—"he'll be back in your arms where he belongs in no time. I know what I'm talking about."

"I'm not good at playing those games," Trisha said curtly, trying to cut the conversation off. She was getting angry with Naomi and was mortified for Strip. Why couldn't Naomi keep her hands out of this?

"Then let me play them for you," Naomi said. "Believe me, I'm a master. Oh, there's Peg. Peg!" she called. "You've done it again! What more can I say?" And, rolling her eyes at Trisha, she hurried away through the crowd.

"Jesus Christ!" Strip said, when Naomi was out of earshot.

"Don't blame me," Trisha said. "Please."

"Do you still love me?" he surprised himself by asking. He thought that all he had been feeling was anger, but a plaintive impulse had broken through. Why am I letting myself in for this? Yet he waited for her reply as though his life depended on it.

"Of course," she said, taking his hand and squeezing it.

"You're not ashamed?"

"Of what?"

"Of me? Of us? Can't you feel people staring? Your son-of-a-bitch husband saw us."

"I know people are staring. I don't mind. I thought I might. I find I rather like it."

"If they're staring that means they're talking too. What d'you think they're saying?" He was so grateful that she had not abandoned him. He wished she could take him in her arms.

"Let them talk," she said. "If they need something to spice up their lives, more's the pity."

"God, I love you," he said. "More than that. I really admire you. You're even better than I thought. Every day you get better than I thought."

"Look at Naomi," Trisha said.

Naomi had edged between Stu and Stacy and was gabbing away at him. Slowly she turned toward Trisha and Strip and, obviously at Naomi's direction, Stu's eyes fell on them from across the room. He said something to Naomi, who nodded, and he looked back at them. Trisha, suddenly oblivious of Strip, smiled over at Stu and gave him an ironic little nod. Then she caught herself and turned to Strip.

"I hope they're enjoying their eyeful," she said.

"You're not trying to make him jealous, are you?"

"Of course not," she said, not pleased with the sound of her own voice. She felt guilty. The truth was, she told herself, she was not entirely

certain of her motives. She could hardly help it
if she took some small pleasure in getting back
at Stu, though from the start of his affair with
Stacy she had felt more contempt for him than
resentment. Strip was so ingenuous. He seemed
to have no trouble always expressing exactly
what was on his mind and in his heart. He
seemed incapable of deception. It was an admirable and endearing quality. The question
was whether it would do him more good than
harm in the world.

Trisha noticed that Dan Santini, big, bronze,
and slick, had entered the gallery. She knew
little about him, except that his business in-
terests were supposed to be faintly suspect, but
immediately she remembered Naomi's telling
her that Stacy and Dan Santini had had lunch
together. Trisha looked over at Stacy and
caught her giving Santini a long, very friendly
stare, as Stu was still buttonholed by Naomi.
Santini returned the look in kind and nodded,
bowing slightly like some two-bit Lothario,
Trisha thought, from a low-budget gangster picture. So that's it, she said to herself. Naomi was
right after all. Poor Stu. He's made such an effort
at playing the rake and now he's about to be let
down with a big thud. I'd be willing to bet that
Stacy leaves this party with Santini. They look
like they deserve each other. Stu's not that type
anyway, underneath. Why is it that men think
they need that kind of woman? Look at him.
He has no idea what's about to happen to him.
This will be a rough evening for him. First me
and Strip and then no Stacy. Suddenly she
heard Strip's voice, realizing that he had been

saying something to her and that she hadn't heard a word. She turned to him.

He looked ghastly. Sweat stood out in large beads on his upper lip, and he looked sick.

"Strip! Are you all right? We'd better step outside."

"Did you hear what I just said?"

"I'm sorry. What was it?"

But Strip looked at her as though he felt ill or horror-struck, she couldn't tell which, and all at once he made for the door, shouldering people out of the way, past Naomi and Stu and out. Trisha stood paralyzed, absorbing the curious, malicious glances of her friends, and then rushed out after him, her champagne glass in her hand.

Fifteen

STRIP ran full speed up La Cienega and was heading down Santa Monica before Trisha had even made it out the door of the gallery. There was no chance she would catch him. He ran and ran, instinctively toward Hollywood, though he no longer lived there, no longer lived anywhere, but he was running from something rather than to anything. Everything about the opening had been hard for him to take, but he could have gotten through all of it if it hadn't been for the last few minutes. He could even have gotten through noticing Trisha's interest in her husband and his girl friend. But when Santini had come in, the boss, the hood, the stinking bastard who, Strip felt certain, had been the man behind Greggie's death—not the hit man but the big man who had ordered it— when Santini had come in looking like the high-rolling, ruthless, slick son of a bitch that he was, at home with those people, Trisha's people, it had been too much. Santini and Rawling's girl friend obviously knew each other too. It had been more than Strip could take, sickening from any angle; and when he had thought about Greggie, thought that what he ought to do was find some way to stick a knife in Santini's throat or at least to call him a killer to his face, there in front of that entire crowd of assholes, knowing that he couldn't do anything at all, not even get Trisha's attention, that had been it.

He ran out of breath in a few blocks and slowed to a walk, a determined-looking walk that had no determination in it. Running had stirred his blood and made him drunker, but now he felt a great thirst and turned into the first bar he came to. The sound of clicking pool balls somehow soothed him. At least he was back on his own turf. That's why I feel this way, he thought. She has her world, I have mine. I'm better off where I belong.

He climbed onto a stool and ordered a draught. The bartender asked for his I.D. He wasn't unfriendly. It was places like this that got raided, Strip thought, not the Beverly Wilshire Hotel. He had never been asked for his I.D. when he had been with Trisha. Just another sign of things, the way they were. Calmly he extracted the perfect duplicate of his brother's driver's license, foolproof, because he and his brother looked alike, and got his beer. He had over fifty dollars in his wallet, he knew. He counted it. Fifty-three. Trisha's money. That would last him until he figured his next move. He sat sipping, calming down, listening to the pool balls. Then he ordered another.

He considered his options. All of his stuff, what little there was, was out at Trisha's. He was sorry about that. This was the point to make a clean break. He would have to see Trisha once more, but he had no choice. He could forget about his stuff—a few T-shirts, a couple of pairs of pants and, oh, yes, his address book—but his car was out there too, and he was in no position to leave that. What would he do? He would find someplace to stay tonight, a cheap motel, then hitch a ride out to the beach tomorrow, collect his car, and split. He saw himself standing before Trisha, explaining that it was all over. Shit, he thought. She would know that.

He shoved his empty glass toward the bartender. Beer here was eighty cents, not too bad a drain on his resources, though if he had twenty-five or thirty, and he felt like it, that would be wasting money. The thing was, where would he go, once he got his stuff? L.A. was becoming claustrophobic. You think you get out of one world and the other one comes back to haunt you. It must have been a hell of a set of coincidences. No, not where money is concerned. Only a few have it. Run into one of them, the others will turn up, one way or another. He would have to try a new place. He had thought of himself as being on his own, but after all, he had never been farther than sixty or eighty miles from his parents' house. New York? He'd have to hitch and he'd be broke by the time he got there. Suicide. San Francisco was a better shot. He imagined himself in San Francisco, looking at the Golden Gate Bridge, and that made him see the ocean and made him think of Trisha, sitting on the beach or running in her mirrors in the moonlight. A lyric ran through his head: You're all wrong but it's all right. Trisha came back to him in full, parts of her, all of her. He could feel her brush running through his hair.

"See this watch?"

It was the guy next to him at the bar. Strip had not been conscious of him until now, and he gave the man a sidelong glance. Forty or so; wearing a T-shirt. A black-nailed index finger pointed to a wristwatch. "How much you'd think I paid f'it." Drunk. "Go on. Guess."

"I don't know," Strip said. "Fifty?"

"Wrong. Nothin'. Not a damn red cent."

"Bargain."

"Damn right. I won it off a guy. Damn fool guy tooka Vikings inna Super Bowl. Cannoo beat that? Vikings. Goddamn Vikings. Wanna beer? C'mon, buya beer."

"No, thanks." Strip drained his glass and left.

Outside the loneliness hit him, and he had a powerful urge to head for the beach and throw himself on Trisha, but he fended it off. He would look for a cheap motel.

He walked and walked. He passed a motel or two but couldn't bring himself to go in. It seemed so futile, spending money probably to lie awake. He passed one that offered X-rated movies. That was all he needed. He realized as he walked that he was pretty drunk, yet he seemed to be able to think clearly. He tripped over his feet a couple of times but the alcohol seemed to be affecting his body more than his head. He couldn't go on walking forever, it occurred to him. What was he going to do? Walk downtown? Walk to Riverside? That would be great. Here I am, Mom and Dad. Defeated.

It was only then that he thought of Nancy. As soon as he did, he wondered why he had not thought of her before. Nancy, who would be there, up on Wilcox, he hoped. He realized that with the certainty of a man who knew his city that if he kept on walking straight long enough he would reach a phone booth. In about ten minutes, he did, outside a Texaco station.

"Hi. It's me, Strip."

"Where are you?"

"I dunno. Somewhere."

"Come on. You high?"

"Drunk. I dunno where I am."

"Yes, you do."

"Just a minute." Strip let the phone hang and ventured out of the booth to the street corner, where he, with intense effort, focused on the sign. He made his way back to the booth, so glad to have made contact with Nancy, sweet Nancy.

"I'm here!"

"Oh, yeah?" Nancy said. "So where is it?"

"It is at the corner of Wilcox and goddamned Santa Monica Boulevard." He was accentuating his syllables like a radio announcer, drunk. "Did you get that? Am I coming in clear?"

"I'll be right there," Nancy said.

She'll be right there, Strip thought, she'll be right there. And she will be, goddamn it. She'll be here, and I'll be there, and everything will be all right. Soon.

It was true. Nancy was there in a couple of minutes, or ten. Strip didn't know the difference. She pulled up in her beat-up Pinto and leaned over to shove the door open. He fell in.

"Good old Strip," Nancy said. "Good old Strip."

They drove in silence the five minutes to her place. That was the great thing, Strip thought in his stupor. No need to say a word. Nancy.

The next morning he awoke on Nancy's couch and contemplated the blanket over him. A nice blanket. He pulled it up around himself. Blanket. Then his mind spread outward. The phone booth. Nancy in the car. He became aware of her apartment. His head lay near the dining-room table, the living-room table. For one second he thought himself at Trisha's and imagined the great expanses of that place: Then he contracted himself back to Nancy's, in the little apartment in the tacky building on Wilcox, where he was. He panicked, he relaxed, panicked again, then realized fully where he was and wondered whether Nancy was still asleep. He felt a surge of feeling toward Nancy. Why did I ever leave Nancy at all? he wondered, and came up with no answer. He fell back to sleep.

When he awoke, Nancy, her long blonde hair falling down, was sitting on the end of the couch, her hand on his blanket-covered feet. Her green eyes were looking at his and as soon as he could form a word he said hello.

"You look like hell," Nancy said. "You look like something awful." It was as though she wanted to kid him but held back, he looked that bad. "What you been doing?"

"I been around," Strip said. "I been to the moon and back."

"As usual," Nancy said. "Coffee?"

"Fantastic." He was absurdly grateful,

188

though he knew he had no reason to be. It shows how screwed up I've been, he thought.

"I met her," Nancy said, bringing the coffee.

"Yeah?" Strip said, taking the steaming cup. "Who?"

"I met the reason you're here. She really fucked you over, didn't she? She came here looking for you."

"You're kidding." He clued in immediately. Trisha had come here that day, following his address book. She had come here looking for him. Much of his warmth toward Nancy dissipated. He was thinking of Trisha now.

"Sure. She was here," Nancy said. "In her Mercedes. She had her friend with her. They were quite a pair. I figured you were in deep. Good old Strip."

Strip could think only of how much Trisha must have wanted to find him, to have followed up this address.

"What'd she say?" he asked.

"Just wanted to know if I'd seen you. I noticed she didn't leave her number," Nancy said. "Didn't surprise me." She gave off a low, warm sound, not a laugh, a sound that said hello, welcome back. Strip didn't want to hear it.

"She say anything else?"

"Nothing else."

He settled down into the couch, pushed this way and that by early-morning emotions. Here was Nancy. I love her, he thought, and he did, and one of the reasons he loved her was that she had been there last night, on the other end of the phone. Another reason he loved her was her hair and the heavy round breasts he knew

waited behind that tunic. Shit, he thought.
What's despair? Ignorance of opportunities.
There was absolutely nothing the matter with
Nancy. He had almost forgotten her skin, one
of those miracles a little bit butterscotch and
so smooth there was no remembering it except
to try to get the tips of your fingers to recall.
So why didn't he want her now? All he knew
was that he didn't.

"You're all fouled up," Nancy said, looking
down at him. He noticed her nose. It had a nice
curve to it. A straight bottom to it, below the
curve. She looked down at him as though she
knew everything he was going through, a little
condescendingly maybe, but with love. What
was it about Nancy?

He didn't care what it was, all of a sudden.
They made love, that was what it was, slow
and easy, good love. She was bigger than he
was, or so it felt. She had her own apartment.
For some reason that thought came to him in
the middle of it. Her own apartment. He went
after her apartment frantically. Her room. Her
telephone. Her body came into it at the end.
And at the very end, herself. His friend. His age.
It was entirely right. He wanted to say, at the
end of it, Where the hell have you been, what
the hell have you been doing? but he stopped
himself and let the misery return. He knew it
was wrong to be doing that, to be thinking about
Trisha then, but he couldn't help it. He hoped
he was concealing it.

"Strip," Nancy said, her face an inch from
his. "Strip. You're still away." She held him to
her. "I don't mind. I know you're carrying some-

thing. Just try to relax. I'm here." She held him tight. She felt incredibly strong and the smell of her sweat was so good it made him hungry.

They ate a big breakfast at Norm's on Vermont. Strip insisted on paying.

"She gave you money?" Nancy asked.

"I got fifty bucks left."

"She give you those clothes too? That's a bad scene, Strip. You don't want to go that way. Get a job, man."

"I know, I know."

"Why d'you think you feel so lousy? She's turning you around, that's why. She's using you. You're her pet."

"Don't say that."

"You're such a romantic. I love you for it but you're killing yourself. Get a job. It's not so bad. I'm just a secretary but I like it."

That was the real reason he had left Nancy, Strip remembered. She was the nicest person in the world but she had low ambitions. Basically, what she wanted was to get married and have about four kids, one after the other. That was all he needed. It would kill him. He'd end up like his father. It was a shame, because Nancy was such a kind, wonderful girl. She wasn't dumb either, and she was beautiful. But the idea of a life of time payments appealed to her. Sure, she'd had her freedom phase, lots of people do. Then they cop out. Maybe it wasn't really copping out. Maybe it was just what they liked, and it probably could mean a happy life if you liked it. It wasn't for him.

"I'm not just romantic, I'm ambitious," he said.

"Sure. But you gottá start somewhere. You'll move up. You run around with your head in the clouds and you're an easy mark for rich women. Rich, bored women looking for a kick."

"I can see why you think that," he said, "but you're wrong. You don't know her."

"I saw her. And her car. And her friend. Her friend looked like the type spends a hundred a week pretending she's not getting old."

Nancy convinced Strip not to go for his stuff right away. She would drive him out there tomorrow or the next day. Tonight she would invite a couple of friends over and they'd have a little party. Nothing big. "We'll mellow out," she said.

Sixteen

TRISHA and Naomi sat at the breakfast table drinking Bloody Marys. Trisha had not returned to the opening after she had run after Strip. She had looked up and down La Cienega; then she had gone to her car feeling down but resigned. There was too much of a gap between them for it to go on any longer, she thought. Everything went well when they were alone, but you could not spend every day alone. She had driven straight back to the beach. The phone had rung about eleven and she had caught herself grabbing for it, hoping it was Strip, but it had been Naomi, wanting to know what had happened and wanting to gossip. Trisha had cut her short and had called the next day to apologize and to invite her down to the beach. There was no point in offending a friend who had her faults but who meant well.

Trisha had lain awake, thinking about Strip, wondering where he was. He never talked about them, but he must have other friends beside Greggie, she thought. She just hoped he hadn't done something crazy, gotten drunker than he must already have been. He was a dear, sweet person, and it had been wrong of her to drag him to the party. She knew the impurity of her motives and she disliked herself for having gone through with it. She had been trying to have it both ways, to carry on what had to be called, however brief, a love affair with Strip and to use him against Stu. It had been exploitive of her and she couldn't recall having done anything like it before, unless it had been in high school or college, and she was disappointed to think herself capable of a juvenile sort of cruelty. Trisha tortured herself with these thoughts late into the night, until they mingled with some pleasurable thoughts of Strip and with plain sadness at losing him. Of course it couldn't have lasted, but if she hadn't been an idiot it could have lasted longer. He would have to come back for his car and his few things. She would try to think of some last speech to say to him, to make him go away believing that she did care for him, that she was genuinely sorry for the pain she had inflicted on him. Poor Strip. How he had made it alone in the world for as long as he had she could hardly understand.

And sensing that Strip was lost to her made her think about Stu. Her feelings toward him were mixed. It was pathetic, the way playing the stud was misfiring for him, but unfortunately Stu's problem had always been finding the right role to play. As for playing himself, that was hard for him. Stu was the sort of guy who tried to do what he thought was expected of him, but who or what was doing the expecting could change from year to year. In the beginning it had been Trisha he had tried to please, but as his business grew he had gotten more and more involved in whatever he thought the successful young executive ought to be doing or having. "We'll have to get one of those," whatever it was, had become a catch-phrase with him: a certain kind of Mercedes, a tennis court. Planning a vacation trip had come for him to mean finding out where the in place was in a given season, and more than once Trisha had felt that he would have been satisfied merely to get his passport stamped and to check in and out of the hotel. Once, she had prevailed upon him to let her pick the spot. She had chosen a place in Mexico she had read about but no one they knew had ever gone to. Stu had tried to put up a brave front, but Trisha could tell that he was disoriented and, under-neath, unable to fathom the purpose of the trip, unless it was to try to start a trend. It was as though the trip would never be valid for him unless, at the very least, some people they knew followed them there and reported back. It was the same way about the sports he took up. Ten-nis was strictly a social enterprise for him. When the running craze started, he got himself outfitted and ran around Bel-Air dutifully for about a week, but that had bored him so in-tensely that he had dropped it. Trisha had been glad that his boredom had forced him to make his own choice.

It was the same with his running around. Trisha knew that he had started it partly be-cause it was the thing to do. You just didn't stick with the same old wife these days, no one did, and there was something wrong with you if you couldn't show you could get young women. In Stu's case Trisha knew it wasn't even the classic middle-aged male doubts. It was worse than that. It was—she hated the expression—peer pressure.

That must have been, she reflected, one of the things that had so attracted her to Strip. Strip seemed to do things only because he wanted to. He was determined to go his own way, yes, even to have his own way, without being domineering about it. He was simply intent, fanatically so, on living his own life, even if it meant violating taboos, crossing lines that were difficult, maybe impossible, to cross. He had never, for instance, made her feel that her being almost twenty years older meant anything to him, except perhaps that it was an attraction, part of the sexual energy between them. But Strip had that rare ability to approach someone strictly as a person, with all the customary means of judgment—age, class, sex—meaning very little to him. Oddly enough, even sexual identity meant little to him in an ordinary way, and when it did, he tried to overcome it. When she thought about it, she had felt more alive with him than at any other time in her life; yet she could not say it was because he had made her feel *more of a woman*, nothing as obvious as that. He had made her feel, their affair had made her feel, more *herself*, whatever that was. More Trisha. God, it was tough and sad to think of being without him!

"Believe me, Trish, you have my sympathy," Naomi said. "You know that."

It was neither what Trisha wanted to hear nor what she wanted. She didn't want anything from Naomi, really, except perhaps her company, and to be honest she wasn't entirely sure about that at the moment. Trisha would have preferred to be alone. Naomi was doing what a friend does, that was all, going on being a friend. She knew that there was not the slightest chance of Naomi's understanding what Strip meant. To her he was just pretty.

"Oh, come on, Naomi, you think I'm a frustrated, love-sick middle-aged woman with a schoolgirl crush on a kid who may be getting off the street by preying on rich women."

"Well, yes, I think it's a possibility. That's why I'm so sympathetic."

"Go on, say it. You think he's my gigolo."

"I wouldn't use that word."

Trisha was angry now. "You couldn't possibly think that if you knew him the way I do," she said.

"My dear, I have no intention of getting to know him the way you do, him or anyone else like him."

"Really, Naomi! What kind of a friend are you? It makes me wonder what you've thought of me all these years if the first time I do something that doesn't fit neatly into established patterns, you try to fit it into one. And an ugly, insulting, sordid one too."

That was the heart of the matter. You know someone and like her for something like fifteen years. You consider her a friend, a best friend even. And then all of a sudden something happens to make you realize she doesn't know you at all, doesn't really trust in your motives, your uniqueness, doesn't even believe what you're saying. Why? Why does this happen? Naomi can't be that bad, Trisha thought. If she is, it says something about me for having trusted her for so long.

Trisha got up, went to the window, looked out. Down the beach a boy was coming out of the water, shaking out his hair. It was not Strip. She wished it were, now. Naomi had stirred her up to the point that she wondered whether Strip had not been right after all. To hell with the world, if this is what the world is. To hell with so-called friends who want to run your life for you. At that moment the idea of living alone with Strip and never seeing anyone at all appealed to her immensely. Now what was she going to do? Living totally isolated, without him, was far less appealing. But how would she ever have the same relationship with people again?

"It doesn't matter if I don't know him," Naomi said. "I know you. And you're just not your old self."

"Thank God for that. I was as bored with that person as Stu was."

Unthinkingly, she had blurted out a truth that made her more sympathetic to Stu. Whatever his faults, she had done little to help them. She had gone along with all of his mindless trendiness, almost always keeping her thoughts to herself. Wasn't that what a good wife was supposed to do? What a joke! What good had it done to understand him and to be understanding to him, when all that did was to make her into a cipher? Sure, she had had an inner life, but the older you get the less important an inner life seemed. What mattered was to have some sort of outer life, one that you could stand or, God help you, even love. I know what I think and what I am inside, she had always told herself. Did Stu know? How could he? All he saw was someone who was so damned co-operative he must have wondered whether he had married a robot. She had always done the "right" thing, and the result was that he had become totally bored with her. She could hardly blame him, when she thought of it like that. She had probably had more disagreements with Strip in a few days than she had had, openly, with Stu during their entire marriage. And, she said to herself with only a trace of guilt, she would trade her entire marriage for that affair. Maybe.

Naomi was not to be stopped yet. She can't, Trisha thought, be expected to read my mind, but she could sure do a better job of under-standing what I'm saying.

"When will they ever find a cure for bore-dom?" Naomi said, still trying to fit Trisha into the cliché. "I'm sorry, Trish, but I can't be of much help in the boredom department." That is certainly true at present, Trisha thought, biting her tongue. "If anything, I'm afraid I aggravate that problem. I just want to help you save your marriage."

"Why?" Trisha shot back at her. "Why do you want to help me save *my* marriage? What do you know about my marriage, really? Were you ever in it? How come you're so sure I wouldn't be better off out of it? I tell you, Naomi, it would be a great help and a consider-able relief if you would stop thinking so obsessively about my marriage and spare a precious thought for me. Myself."

"Okay then, *my* marriage. Haven't you ever heard of the domino theory applied to marriage? One couple in a crowd splits up, then another." Naomi made a wide gesture with her hands, trying to indicate something approximating the fall of the Roman Empire.

"I certainly don't want to endanger your marriage," Trisha said, "but I'm afraid that if Stu and I stay together or get divorced it won't be because we're thinking of you and Al. Isn't that asking a bit much?"

"I'm just trying to be honest."

"You don't think your marriage is really in any danger, do you? My God. You and Al will still be married after they abolish the institution. Al would go to pieces without you, and you obviously don't want to leave. What are you worried about?"

"You make it sound like there's something the matter with me for wanting to stay married. You're talking like some kind of radical feminist. I suppose the next thing, you'll be in favor of self-insemination."

"I'm sorry, Naomi. I didn't mean it that way. Of course I don't think there's anything the matter with wanting to stay married. Just remember, I wasn't the one who started fooling around in my marriage. It's just that, when certain things happen, it becomes difficult or impossible to imagine they could ever be the same again."

"Maybe they could be better," Naomi said, trying everything.

"Maybe."

They were at an impasse. Trisha's anger had dissipated, but she knew that she and Naomi were not really communicating, all because, Trisha thought, Naomi refused to admit any real value to the affair with Strip. But after all, she could be acting worse: She could be scandalized or pretend to be.

"Not to put too great a strain on an old friendship," Naomi said, "but I'd like another drink."

"Sure."

Naomi followed Trisha into the kitchen, came up to her and put an arm around her. "All right," she said, "let me try another tactic. None of your friends will ever trust you with their teen-age sons if you continue with this outrageous and bizarre behavior."

That raised a laugh. Trisha decided to have another drink too. It was warming up outside. They would go out on the deck.

The sea was rough that day and at first the effort of raising their voices above the waves did not seem worth it, so they sat contemplating the surf. Not talking made Trisha's spirits sink. Her emotions had been pulled in so many directions. She was normally a person very much in control of herself. Coming down to the beach to begin with, she remembered, deciding to be alone to think about her marriage, she had not been terribly distraught. She had lost a little sleep, that was all. But now she seemed to be experiencing depression and anxiety in rapid succession. Strip had really gotten to her. Was it possible that she cared more for him than for anything else?

"It can't last," Naomi said, apropos of nothing. Trisha wished Naomi would let the whole subject drop, impossible though that was.

"No one ever said Stu and I wouldn't last," Trisha said.

How irrelevant that standard, endurance, seemed to Trisha now! What was it about people that made them judge everything by the standard of longevity? Her own parents' marriage had lasted nearly half a century, owing chiefly to just the right combination of religion and Scotch whiskey, and she didn't envy it. Endurance was an admirable quality, but so was brevity, the brief, spectacular flowering, and a capacity for change. Strip was a lost soul in many ways, but would he have been better off enduring the life of his family? The answer was obvious enough. And, she reminded herself, she was not responsible for the state of her marriage, and if she was, it was precisely because she had been too patient, too enduring, too willing to put up with the routine and the mediocre. You couldn't win.

Out on the Coast Highway Nancy was dropping Strip off and giving him some advice. He was not to allow himself to be used by this woman any longer. And he was to know that he always had a place to stay.

"You can stay with me as long as you like," Nancy said. "Don't forget that. Don't ever feel you're desperate, okay?"

"Okay," Strip said. "I'll be in touch."

"You coming back this evening?"

"I don't know. Probably. I'll call."

He made his way toward Trisha's and noticed a car parked in front. He thought he recognized it as Naomi's but he wasn't sure and since, naturally, it was a Mercedes, it could have been anyone's. It was going to be hard enough to see Trisha again without having to confront Naomi too. Since the gallery opening Strip had decided that however much Trisha was to blame for what had happened, Naomi was more at fault, for meddling, for trying to stir up trouble, for trying to get Stu's attention. Trisha had her faults, but she was superior to her friends, Strip had decided, and left on her own, away from that no-good crowd, she was as close to perfect as anyone he had ever met. The trouble was, no one ever seemed to be left on their own, except him.

He decided to scout around, to try to see whether it was Naomi in there. If so, he would probably hide out until she left. He made his way down along the side of the house. They were probably out on the deck.

He had not enjoyed himself especially at Nancy's. The little party she had thrown had been all right. They had sat around smoking and drinking wine and listening to some tapes. One guy had fooled around with a pack of Tarot cards. The usual. Strip had felt out of it. He could not get Trisha off his mind for a minute and he had pretended to get high just so as not to have to talk to anyone. He had thought of a thousand things he wanted to say to Trisha and had been tormented by one image after another of her. The longer he was away from her, the more he wanted her, the more he thought up excuses and forgiveness for her. You can't stay married to a guy for that long, he had told himself, thinking of Trisha and Stu, and not be pissed off if he's running around. He reminded himself that he always felt at least a little jealous when he saw an old girl friend with somebody else, even if he hadn't the least desire to be with her himself. Trisha had only been acting human.

He had thought he had gotten used to being on his own, but now he felt incomplete without Trisha. Sitting there in Nancy's apartment, with the music playing and the talk drifting aimlessly from James Taylor to the Middle East to the price of hash, his spirits dropped lower and lower, and he pretended to pass out on the couch, just so he could close his eyes, turn his face to the wall, and hang on. He told himself over and over that everything with Trisha was finished; at the same time he wanted with every cell in his being to be with her, and the tension between his resolve and his impulses was something awful. When everyone had left, Nancy had come over to him and touched him gently on the shoulder. She had wanted him to come into her bed. But he pretended to be dead to the world, and eventually she had gone to bed by herself, after covering him with a blanket and kissing him. He felt grateful to her, but he knew that she was incapable of understanding anything of what he was feeling.

Now he crept along the side of the house, making his way down to the beach, beside the sundeck. A wave broke, and as it rushed in, he heard voices.

"How on earth will you explain Strip to Tim?" Naomi was saying. "Have you thought of that?"

"Of course" came Trisha's voice. "All the time. I'm not saying it could last with Strip. I never thought it would. I wasn't ready for it to end just yet, that's all."

"Well, you've had your desirability reaffirmed. Isn't that enough? I'm sure that's what hooked you."

A wave broke over Trisha's reply. Strip was frustrated not to hear it, but then, he told himself, maybe it was better that he couldn't. He was beginning to feel like running. He could take his car and forget the rest. Then Trisha's voice could he heard again.

"He was so needful. He has nothing. Nobody. I couldn't turn him away. He'd just lost his best friend. He was so lost. I don't know. He touched me, somehow. I wanted to help him."

"But it's over now, isn't it? You'll tell him? When he comes back?"

"I think he already knows."

That was enough for Strip. He ran to his car.

Seventeen

THE dogs had heard the car start and had started yipping and running toward the front door.

"That's probably Strip," Trisha said.

"I'll be going," Naomi said.

"You don't have to."

"Don't be silly. I may be a busybody, but I'm not entirely without common sense. Good-bye, love. And good luck. I do hope it's not too painful." She gave Trisha a kiss and they went to the front door.

But Strip's car was gone.

"I guess that's that," Naomi said.

"I don't know where to send his things," Trisha said. "You can stay now, if you like." Her manner lacked enthusiasm.

"You probably want to be alone. Now keep calm, and everything will cheer up in a few days. I can guarantee you Stu will be here on his hands and knees before long. You should have seen him when Stacy left the opening with Dan Santini. I mean, he tried to put up a front but—"

"I don't want to hear about it, Naomi."

"Of course not. Bye-bye."

Trisha went up to her bedroom. She had a compulsion to gather Strip's things up. Or did she just want to see them, since she had missed seeing him? That he had taken his car

211

and gone, that she might well never see him again, these were realities that were crowding in on her mind, clouding it over the way steam clouds a mirror, but she was trying still to push them away.

She opened the bureau drawer she had given him, cleaned out the few shirts, the jeans, the socks and underwear, and the swimming trunks, and piled them on the bed. She took his suitcase out of the closet, put it on the bed, and methodically began putting the clothes in it. Then she broke down. She threw herself onto the bed and sobbed into the pillow, irrationally trying to stifle the sound, as though someone might hear.

Later, more or less in control, she performed every household chore she could think of, tidying up, feeding the dogs, sweeping the deck. And all the while she thought, There is a purpose in doing all this. It is necessary to do this. But it would be so much nicer to have someone to do them for. I can be alone. Maybe I'll be alone from now on. But I don't want to be alone. Being alone is just being.

When there was nothing more to do, she made some tea, turned on the television, and picked up a book. The words were on the page, but they didn't mean anything, and the television was just noise. She tried to remember whenever she had felt this low before. It had been just after she had lost her baby. No, that had been worse. Nothing could ever be as bad as that. For a moment the thought comforted her, that things could be worse than this, but then it was as though the baby had just died.

This is why people have religion, she thought. If things go on like this, I'm going to get it too. I'll end up an old woman in church.

Strip had reached Santa Monica before any thought had formed clearly in his head. He had driven from Malibu to Santa Monica in a daze, not seeing anything, and when he came to, his first impulse was to find a bar, but he didn't want to do that, he decided. That would put him right back where he had been, and he would be back at Nancy's as confused and miserable as ever. Something within made him get hold of himself. An impulse similar to Trisha's for tidying up made him crave to get his mind and his emotions in order and, since he had no idea where he was going or what he was doing, he decided to pretend he did, to act like a normal person going somewhere. What did you do when you were going somewhere? Well, eventually, you pulled off the road and you ate a meal. So he did.

It was just a hamburger place, but he considered the menu seriously, making the choice between fries and onion rings important. He decided on the cheeseburger with onion rings.

"Are the onion rings fresh-made or frozen?" he asked the waitress.

"I don't know."

"Well, could you find out? If they're frozen, I want the fries."

He got the fries. They were frozen too, but it mattered more with the onion rings. As he picked up a fry in his fingers and dabbed it into some ketchup, he noticed that his hand was trembling. It's a good thing I didn't start in on the beer, he told himself.

He stayed in the restaurant a long time, drinking coffee. Halfway though his fourth cup he reached a decision. He would go back and get his things. And he would make a last, calm speech to Trisha, telling her that she was a fine person and that he was grateful to her for taking him in. He had himself together now, and he was going to be all right on his own. He would never forget her, and he hoped that she would always have a few fond memories of him. Good-bye. That was what he would say to her.

When Trisha heard his knock she leaped out of her chair and made it to the door in a few long strides. She flung it open and threw her arms around him. But he was rigid and cold and did not respond. That brought her to her senses. She had forgotten that it was all over.

"I came for my things," he said.

"Of course."

The dogs were their usual frantic selves, and as soon as he was inside, Strip bent down to examine Corky's leg. He removed the bandage and announced that it could be left off, there was no need for further treatment.

"Can I get you a cup of tea?"

"No. I had too much coffee."

"Anything?"

"No."

"Well, come in and sit down for a minute. We don't have to pretend we don't know each other."

Just that was enough to make Strip want her,

but he suppressed the feeling and took a seat on the couch. Trisha switched off the TV and sat in her chair, opposite him.

"You don't have a fire," he said.

"I didn't bother."

"It's getting cold out."

"Do you want me to make one? I will."

"No."

Strip went over his speech in his mind. But this didn't seem the right moment for it. He had not counted on being seated, for one thing. And maybe she had a speech too. He would wait and see.

"Why did you run away?" Trisha asked. "From the opening."

"A lot of reasons."

"Was it seeing my husband that upset you? Did I upset you?"

"I wasn't upset. I was disgusted. I been disgusted before. I'll get over it."

Trisha came over and sat down on the floor next to him, her legs curled under her. She reached up to take his hand, but he dropped his head and held it in his hands.

"Don't," he said.

"Strip, why were you so disgusted? You think I was using you? I really wasn't. If I was at all, I'm sorry. I just wanted to be with you."

"Why don't you wake up!" His tone was sharp. "Come out and play in the real world. You don't know nothin' about what's going on. Right in front of your nose and you don't see it."

She drew back. "You don't have to rub it in about my husband's having an affair."

"Rub it in! That bozo. He was tryin' to make time with any chick'd look at him. Always has. I knew that back in my valet days. You'd be surprised what you could learn about people just from parkin' their cars. Maybe you oughta try it."

Trisha got up and went into the kitchen. Strip sat there, wondering at the words that had just escaped his mouth. Why had he said them? This wasn't the way he wanted it to be at all. He had come in depressed, resigned, yet still full of love for her, and now this flash of anger. Where had it come from? From the kitchen he heard the sound of Trisha softly blowing her nose. He had made her cry. This was all wrong. He got up and went to her.

"Look," he said, "I'm really sorry. I was makin' all that up. Honest. I don't know why I said it. I don't know why I'm so ticked off. I don't want you to cry."

"I don't know why you're angry either," she said. "And I still don't really know why you left the party. I can guess at it. I know you felt out of place, and I wasn't paying enough attention to you. And yes, I got some pleasure, maliciously, from having my husband see you with me. I'm sorry about that."

"That's okay."

"Let's sit down and have a reasonable conversation."

They went to the couch together. Trisha put her arm around him and stroked his hair.

"I don't know," Strip said. "I was drinkin' too much, for one thing. It was all too much for me. I figured everybody was lookin' down at me. Which they did. I'm right about that, aren't I?"

"Maybe. But I thought they were looking at us, not just you. Remember? I told you I didn't mind it."

"Okay. But there was somethin' else. That really did it."

"What?"

"Santini."

Trisha was nonplussed. She could not imagine why Strip would care about Santini and Stacy. She said nothing, and he explained how Greggie had told him about Santini and had always referred to him as "Mr. Main Event"; Santini was probably the biggest guy in the illegal drug traffic in the city; Santini, Strip knew, was the one who ordered Greggie killed. Naturally, he hadn't done the job himself. Those guys never do. They paid somebody or found some guy they had something on.

"What can I do?" Trisha said. She was horrified and she was certain, somehow, that Strip knew what he was talking about. "Do you want me to do something?"

"You? I don't see nobody can do anything. He's dead. If you're thinkin' about exposin' Santini, forget it. Nobody'll ever get him. He's got too much on too many people. Besides, who cares about a dead kid that was in up to his neck anyway? Nobody."

Trisha was trying to assimilate it all. She had had no idea, of course. Here she had been trying to figure out Strip's behavior strictly on the

217

basis of his reaction to herself and Stu. She felt foolish and guilty. Of course he had run away. Who wouldn't have?

"I just wish you'd taken me outside and told me then," she said. "It might have saved us both a lot of anguish."

"Yeah . . . I better have that picture of me and Greggie. I decided I better send it to his parents. You think that'll upset 'em?"

"I'm sure they'd like all the pictures of him they could have. Are they nice people?"

"They're all right. Me and Greggie, we used to go out and eat there some of the time. When funds got low. Which was usually."

Trisha suggested that Strip give them the picture in person. He said that he would think about it, but that he was reluctant to tell them the truth about Greggie's life and death.

"I can see why," Trisha said, and she drew him toward her. "Strip. Let's talk about us."

He pulled away, got up, and walked around. He looked at the photograph of Tim and his parents. Then he turned to Trisha, looking down at her.

"Let's face facts," he said. "There ain't no us. Not anymore." He let this sink in. "I been tryin' to find a way to put it. There's nothin' to say. I gotta get out. I'm really only here for my stuff. And to say goodbye."

Trisha could not look at him now. She slumped down.

"No way it would've worked, right?" he went on. "I mean, you was always out of my reach. Who am I kidding?" Trisha still said nothing, still sat with her head down. "Besides, pretty soon you'll be old enough to be my grandmother."

She got up at this barb and walked to the window, looking out, unable to see anything but her own reflection and Strip's behind her. Of course he's right, she thought. But why do I feel this way, as though my heart were being ripped out? She watched in the window as Strip came up behind her. Let him put his arms around me, she thought.

"Nothin' ever works out anyway," he said, tenderly now. "So what's the point? I gotta leave."

"Where will you go? What will you do?"

Strip paced around the room. With a rush of bravado he announced that there were a million things he could do. Trisha looked at him, waiting for him to be a little more specific. He felt the pressure and began expanding.

"Well, there's Vegas," he started. "There's all kinds of bread there. I'm not talkin' peanuts. I mean megabucks, lots and lots, if you know what I mean. I gotta hook up with the right operation, that's all. People get rich quick there. It happens."

"Strip."

He pushed on. "I could hook up with a rich woman. Just the other night this lady asks me would I go someplace with her. Someplace. I can't remember. She wasn't bad-lookin' either. Younger than you."

"How lucky for you."

"Don't get me wrong. There's opportunities

all over. I got this movie offer. A skin flick. I'm
still considerin' that. Course I don't want to do
nothin' too, you know."

She looked at him coldly.

"You're right. I got too much false pride, like
you said. Anyway, Vegas is my best bet. What's
the matter? Why are you lookin' at me that
way? I'm a nice boy!"

"You must be pretty frantic. And you must
be in a lot of pain yourself. To want to hurt me
like that now."

The telephone. For once Trisha was glad of
it. She went into the kitchen to answer it.

"Oh. Hello, Stu." Strip could hear Trisha's
voice. Stu was asking about coming out to see
her. "Not tonight. No." she said. He had felt
bad about seeing her at the gallery opening. "I
felt bad too." Why couldn't he come out tonight?
"It wouldn't be a good idea."

Now Stu was suspicious. He accused Trisha
of having someone at the house. His voice rising, he asked what going on with her. Everyone
at the party had been talking. It was horribly
embarrassing. How old was that kid, anyhow?

"About Stacy's age, I'd say. Why?"

Stu said that she ought to know why. All
right. So they had both been foolish. But it was
worse for her.

"For me?" Trisha asked, her voice heavy with
sarcasm. "For a woman? That's what you
mean, isn't it? Look, not tonight. We can talk
tomorrow." She hung up. As she did, she heard
Strip's steps hurry down the stairs and into the
hallway. She heard the door open and shut. He's

been up to get his things, she thought. He'll have seen them all packed and won't understand. She tried to run to stop him, but as she opened the door, he drove away.

Eighteen

WHEN Stu called the next day, Trisha again refused to talk to him. When was she going to talk, he wanted to know, and she said she had no idea. The last thing she wanted was to talk to him when she was feeling so vulnerable, and his remark about Strip's age, the snide way he had referred to it, still burned. Stu had been dumped by Stacy, so he was anxious to come running back. Well, he could wait. There were times when she thought it would be best for him to wait forever. At other times she came close to calling him, when she was feeling especially anxious and desperate. It was then she remembered some of the good things about Stu that it had been so hard to think about lately, and it was then that the more pleasant memories of their marriage came back to her, times together with Tim, times spent enjoying the beach house. But she kept these thoughts at bay. She knew she was in no shape to make any decisions or judgments.

She fended Naomi off too for a couple of days, and then agreed to meet her for lunch at the Cafe Swiss. That was a mistake. Trisha could think about nothing but Strip in that restaurant. She had agreed to go there at Naomi's suggestions: When it occurred to her that it might be painful, she dismissed the notion. Was she going to go around avoiding every place they had been together? Besides, she couldn't think of an excuse not to go there. They sat inside where it was cool and dark, and she kept glancing out at the patio, as though looking for Strip's ghost.

"You're still not yourself, Trish," Naomi said. "I can't believe you're pining after that boy."

"Naomi, we really ought to talk about something else. There's no chance you'll ever understand about that. I'm not going to try to convince you any more."

"Maybe I'm missing something."

"Maybe you are."

The attempts at other topics did not go very far, and Trisha found herself glancing at her watch to see whether she had been there long enough to have fulfilled what had turned out to be a social obligation. She and Naomi would be close again, she felt, fairly close at any rate. There would always be, it seemed, a large part of her heart that she would never be able to share, not with Naomi or anyone else.

Everything had gone stale. She found herself uncharacteristically listless. Hours would pass without her accomplishing anything. Even the house began to go to hell, until she forced herself to put things in order. Tim was due home in a couple of weeks and she was worried about that. She wouldn't have to explain Strip now, but how would she explain her mood? She imagined asking Tim about himself and his plans and not really caring what he said. He would sense that. She found herself scanning her bookshelves for stories about broken love affairs, reading them for advice, as though they were guidebooks. She read *The Doctor's Wife* by Brian Moore, a novel about a woman who goes to France and has a passionate affair with a much younger man. Her husband arrives to take her away, but she defies him. Then the youth turns out to be something of a jerk, and she leaves him. But she does not go back to her husband. I don't know, Trisha thought, I don't know. She knew it was ridiculous for her to read books in this way, but she didn't know what else to do. She kept thinking that each day would bring some resolution, but almost two weeks had passed and none came.

She decided to take up tennis again and made an appointment to resume her lessons at the club. But when she arrived there a few days later, she found that she had come a day early. The instructor, tall and muscular, made a stupid remark about her being so eager to see him, grabbing her arm and leering at her. She wrenched free and hurried away, saying to herself that that was the end of the tennis lessons for a while. Anything even remotely sexual repelled her. Another time, in another life, she thought, I might have found that amusing. Maybe I will again.

One day she was returning from a walk with the dogs on the beach, picking up the odd piece of trash here and there. Bending down, she noticed the glint of a green wine bottle that had been worked into the sand up under the sun deck. The bottle had a cork sticking out of it. She retrieved it and, holding it up to the light, saw that it contained a folded piece of paper. She sat down on the sand, hesitating. Obviously this was Strip's. But was it the original bottle she had watched him throw out or a new one? Had he been back to leave a note? She came alive at the possibility. She still had his address book. He had run out without it finally, as always, but he had not been able to bring himself to claim it again. Maybe he had come back and lost heart and left a note instead. What would the note say? "Meet me at . . ." or "I love you . . ."?

She could not hold back any longer. She smashed the bottle on a rock and opened up the note:

WHAT A WORLD!

She was touched and a little disappointed too. It had to be his original note. He had not come back. Then she remembered a very high tide a couple of days before: It must have brought the bottle in and washed it clear up under the deck. What a world. Strip's words. She looked at the lettering and held back tears. What a kid. Her heart filled with longing and good feeling toward him, as she read this message from a lost child over and over. I'll always keep it, she thought.

The note haunted her. She kept it on her bedside table and could not stop staring at it. What was wrong, she had begun to think, was not so much that they had ended the affair. There was no way to figure that it could last, although it could have lasted longer, maybe a lot longer. What was wrong was the way it had ended. Drama. A burst of emotion. Strip's understandable immaturity and his immense pride and fragile ego all combining to demand all or nothing, coming up with nothing, quickly. They had really just been getting to know each other. Her feelings for him were at their peak when the break had come. It was unreal.

They had come to care for one another as people, hadn't they? And then in a night, it was over. That was why she could not seem to get it into perspective or get her feelings in order. It was one thing to go on caring for someone; it was another to be in a state of emotional chaos with no sign of its diminishing. She looked at the note for the thousandth time and thought, I am going to have to do something.

Strip had gone to Nancy's. He had not wanted to, but he couldn't think of anything else. At first she assumed that he had taken her advice and made a clean break, and he was content to let her think that. She congratulated him, told him that he could get himself straightened out. He could stay as long as he liked. Maybe he should start thinking about getting a job, but he didn't have to rush it.

He tried to let his despair take over only in the daytime, when Nancy was at work. He would make some gestures at cheerfulness, perhaps, a self-deprecating joke about his not wanting to sleep with her, and see Nancy off to work. She didn't seem to mind his lack of sexual interest in her, but he figured that if he stayed on much longer, it would become an issue. Once Nancy was out of the apartment, he would collapse on the couch and go over his options. There did not see to be any. Thoughts

of Trisha would assail him, mix with fears of
the future, and by ten o'clock he was a mass of
anxiety and longing. He would turn on the
television and watch game shows and soaps
until the middle of the afternoon, never going
out. This is how my mother ended up, he
thought. He did stay away from drink. He was
certain of what that would do to him if he gave
in to it.

Nancy would come home and ask him what
he had been up to.

"I been goin' through the want-ads," he would
lie. Sometimes he would mark up the newspaper at random, to make it look as though he
had been searching.

"Find anything?"

"Not yet. I made a couple phone calls. One
guy said he thought he might have somethin'
for me. Call me back."

"What sort of job?"

"Let's see. Selling encyclopedias, I think it
was."

"You can do better than that."

"Yeah. That's what I figured."

After days and days of this he felt he had to
do something. He had one piece of unfinished
business, Greggie's parents. He would go talk
to them. He would think of something to tell
them. It would get him out of the apartment.

He made his way out to the Pomona Freeway
and Highway 60 concocting stories. An auto-
mobile accident in another state. A mysterious
disease. Drowning, that was it. They had been
surfing. Greggie had been hit on the head with
his board and had gone under. There was a

terrific undertow that day and evidently his body had been pulled out to sea. He had never been found. The Coast Guard, everybody tried, but it was his sad duty to inform them that Greggie was dead.

He drove around the block a couple of times, getting his courage up, rehearsing his story, and then he found himself facing the McAlisters. They looked the same as ever, worn, maybe a little more worn than usual. Greggie was their only child. This was going to be rough.

"We're so glad you came," Mrs. McAlister said. She pressed him into her big, soft body. "We were hoping you would, after we heard about Greggie. We know how much you loved him."

"That's right," Mr. McAlister said. "We were worried about you too, after what happened."

So they already knew. How much? Strip wondered. Everything?

Greggie had given his parents' name to the police as soon as he had been booked.

"We saw him in jail, you know, the very next day. Out at Beverly Hills," Mrs. McAlister said.

"You did? He talked to you?"

"Yes," she said. "He told us everything. He told us soon as he was arrested, he decided he was goin' to tell us everything. It weren't a very pretty story, but we was proud of him for tellin' us."

"He was goin' to come back here," Mr. McAlister said, "soon as he got out. Take a job in my shop, save a little cash, then maybe try somethin' else. Somethin' on the right side of the law. He was through with them crooks. He told us you'd been tryin' to get him to get free of that crowd."

"We're very grateful to you for that, Strip," Mrs. McAlister said, and she threw her arms around him again. She and Strip had a good, deep cry together, while Mr. McAlister stood by and watched.

Strip stayed for supper. The McAlisters were deeply religious people, and they talked about how Jesus was helping them in their crisis. Their minister had been helpful. The thing they were most grateful for was that Greggie had decided to change at the end. They had never known anything about his activities. They had worried about him, but they had known he had a good friend in Strip, and Greggie had always been a good boy.

"It's easy to get in with the wrong people," Strip said. He was feeling very emotional, toward the McAlisters but also toward Trisha. He wanted to phone her and tell her how things had come out, but he figured it would be a mistake.

After supper, while Mrs. McAlister did the dishes, Strip and Mr. McAlister talked over coffee. How was Strip getting along?

"Pretty good. I'm goin' pretty good, Mr. McAlister."

"What you doin'?"

"Oh, I'm out of a job just now. But something'll turn up soon."

"You know, you can always have a job in

my shop. You could live here too, if you want. Greggie's room."

Strip thanked Mr. McAlister warmly but declined, recoiling immediately from the idea, but saying he would certainly keep it in mind and he intended to stay in touch. After that, Mr. McAlister said nothing, and they sat in silence until Mrs. McAlister came out and Strip got up to leave.

"Did you tell him, Tom?" she asked her husband.

"Yup. He says he'll think about it."

"Do, Strip. We mean it. We could help you out. Greggie never had to leave, you know. But he had some idea of getting rich quick. We tried to tell him, Save a little, put some aside, go to school maybe, then go on your own. But he wouldn't listen. You think about it."

He did, though it seemed an awful comedown for his ambitions. Mr. McAlister's metal shop was a pretty puny operation, and Strip hated the idea of moving back to Riverside. But he did go back, after considering his options again for a few more days. He would be able to save practically his entire salary, because he knew that the McAlisters would not let him pay for anything, and in a few months, he would have a bankroll. By that time he would have figured what to do with it.

He was grateful to the McAlisters, but one of the reasons he accepted their offer was that he knew he would be doing them some good too. He would be their second son.

Nineteen

TRISHA wanted to see Strip. Once she accepted that this was what she really wanted her mood changed and she was able to sleep almost through the night again. She got the house in order. She was able to talk to Naomi on the phone and to put Stu off without anxiety or anger. She guessed—she was not willing to go further than that—that she and Stu would be back together eventually, but she had determined at least that a longer separation was necessary. Tim would just have to accept that his parents were having some problems and he could stay in Bel-Air or at the beach when he came home, as he chose. If any of his friends, for some of them were the sons and daughters of people Trisha knew, gossiped about her, that would have to be the way it was.

She felt sure that she would be able to find Strip. She guessed that he would not be able to put off confronting Greggie's parents very long. He was too responsible and cared too much for other people's feelings to back out of that task, however unpleasant it would be for him. She thought of telephoning the McAlisters: Their address and phone number were in Strip's meticulously kept address book. She had thumbed through the book often: That, the note, and the photograph were all she had left of Strip. Each time she looked at the book, she saw his per-

sonality written there in the way he had made
the careful entries. With scarcely an address
to call his own, those of other people were vital
to him, and he clung to them as to a raft. Yet
he was always leaving the book with her. That
said something too, something it choked her up
to think about.

She knew only that she wanted to see him
again, not how often. She knew the affair could
not last, did not even consider wanting it to go
on indefinitely, but at the same time she knew
now that there was no reason to end their
friendship as though one of them had contracted a fatal, communicable disease. She also
had a strong urge to help him along in life in
some way. It was not flattering to her to think
that they had been so close and that he had
left her life just as lost, just as aimless as he
had come into it. She had failed him there,
definitely. She wasn't thinking of giving him an
allowance or anything like that, but she ought
to be able to make some kind of difference in
his life. He had made one in hers, she now
realized. She was not the same person she had
been, or rather, she was more herself, even as
she had been when she had been with him. She
was more confident; she found it easier to say
no to people, including, most especially, to Stu.
And yes, she had a confidence in her sexuality
that she had not had before. Nothing so banal
as having her "desirability reaffirmed," as
Naomi had so clumsily put it: more that there
was now a harmonious union between her sexuality and her self-confidence.

Yet she had no desire for sex, except when

she thought of Strip. One of the reasons she was putting off any decisions about Stu was that she knew, if a reunion with him was going to work, that she would have to sleep with him, and she could not face that now. It was not that she was repelled; it was that she had no desire for him. And one of the consequences of her self-confidence was that she now felt no need to act without desire. One day she would probably desire Stu again, but she was not going to force it.

When she contemplated telephoning the McAlisters, something put her off. It seemed too impersonal. What she would do would be to go out and talk to them, maybe arrange to see Strip through them. She had a hunch that he might be taking an occasional meal out there, as he used to do with Greggie. Just on the chance, she decided she would visit them on a Sunday: Strip might be there. They would be the sort of people who had a big dinner on Sunday afternoon. All of this was speculation, but somehow she sensed she was guessing right. He was gone, but it was as though there were an invisible bond between her and Strip, a navigational beam that would lead her to him, one way or another. She looked at a calendar and next Sunday's date fairly leaped at her. It was Strip's birthday! She could hardly believe the perfect timing. This would be one birthday Strip would enjoy.

So on September 4th, Trisha found herself on the Pomona Freeway and Highway 60, following the signs to Riverside. She had maps too. She had prepared for the journey as though it were an important expedition—as indeed it was—consulting the auto club, getting the car washed. She had debated what to wear and had changed clothes several times, scrutinizing herself in the mirror. Nothing seemed quite right, until she tried on the mirrored caftan. Maybe it wasn't appropriate to meet the McAlisters, but she knew Strip loved it, and he might be there. With it she wore sandals, her legs bare.

It was a longer trip than she had imagined, a good two hours from Malibu, and by the time she arrived on the streets of Riverside, her eyes were smarting from the smog. Riverside has its attractive sections, but the McAlisters did not live in one of them. Magnolia Avenue, Third Street. She checked her map and eventually she found herself opposite the house, and was shocked.

Somehow she had expected to find a tidy little bungalow, maybe something like a miniature farmhouse, but what she saw was an aluminum-frame stationary mobile home. There were other mobile homes on the street and of them this was perhaps the best kept, but it was obviously very old and ready for the scrap heap. The whole street was the same, big dogs wandering about, shabby houses, cars and pickups parked all over the place, some abandoned on scruffy lawns. Trisha's Mercedes could not have been more incongruous.

Nor could she herself have been, when she stepped out of her car. And she was observed. A touch football game stopped. Beer cans were held poised in the air. Many of the people of the neighborhood were outside on this warm Sunday in early September, and Trisha wondered what on earth they thought she was doing there. A rich aunt come to visit? Not too far off the mark. She locked the car.

Mrs. McAlister came to the door.

"Hello, Mrs. McAlister? My name is Trisha Rawlings. I'm a friend of Strip Harrison's. I wonder if you could help me find him. I have a couple of things for him and I've lost track of his address."

"Strip? He lives here now."

"He does?" Trisha was delighted, excited, but also concerned. She did not like to think of Strip having to live here, and she wondered why he was. Was he ill?

"He's been here two weeks. Won't you come in? You can wait for him if you like. Him and my husband, they're down at the market. Should be back soon."

"Thank you."

Trisha made her way into the tiny living room and tried to take it in. An aquamarine carpet; a Formica-topped table and matching chairs; on one wall a framed commercial photograph of Yosemite National Park and on another a sampler, saying "He Is Risen." On top of a big color television was a knick-knack shelf holding a plaster ballerina, a ceramic cocker spaniel, and a collection of spoons marked with the seals of major American cities. And in a free-standing frame, a photograph of Greggie.

"Why don't you just rest yourself on the couch, Mrs. Rawlings. Like some coffee?"

"I'd love some."

"Iced tea?"

"That would be even better. Thank you."

The place was clean, she noticed. She felt somehow enormous in it.

"You're from Los Angeles, I'll bet," said Mrs. McAlister, bringing in the tea. "You've known Strip a while?"

There was something a little suspicious in Mrs. McAlister's manner, Trisha thought. Maybe Strip told her all about Greggie and she thinks I'm somebody from the underworld.

"Not too long, actually," Trisha said. "A few weeks. Strip, ah, was at a party at my house. We have some mutual friends. We sort of got to know each other. I think he's wonderful, don't you?"

"Oh, Strip's the best, the very best. He works for my husband now, you know."

"Does he? What does he do?"

"Metalwork. My husband has a metal shop. Small jobs, repairs, things like that."

Trisha regarded Mrs. McAlister. She was large, fat even, floury-faced, yet pleasant looking. "I didn't know Strip had a talent for that kind of work," Trisha said.

"You know, Tom, my husband, he says Strip's just a very good worker. Says he came in not knowing a thing, and he's already the best worker in the shop. We got three others, or two, I forget."

"A thriving business."

"Well, we get by."

She thought Mrs. McAlister was warming up a bit, but she wanted to get on closer terms with her, before Strip came back, so there would not be any suspicions about his mysterious visitor.

"Mrs. McAlister," she began, "I know about Greggie. I'm terribly sorry."

"You knew Greggie?"

"No, I didn't. I wish I had, from what Strip says about him. Strip was devastated by what happened, I suppose you know. That's really, in a way, how we got to know one another, Strip and I. He came to me. I don't know, for some reason he thought he could confide in me. He was at loose ends, really. And I—listened to him and maybe gave him some comfort."

"That was good of you. More iced tea?"

"Thanks. It's delicious."

Trisha could tell that things would be all right now between her and Mrs. McAlister.

"You know," Mrs. McAlister said when she returned, "this has been a terrible thing that's happened to us, Mrs. Rawlings."

"Trisha."

"Trisha. My name's Margie. Or Marge. Just terrible. I don't suppose there's anything worse than losing your only son. Now I know how people felt in wartime. I can't imagine anything worse."

"I agree." Trisha saw that Mrs. McAlister—Margie—was near tears.

"But you know, it's been a kind of a miracle, Strip's coming here. He's taken Greggie's place, you see. It's a kind of a miracle, almost as good as getting our son back. I think Jesus sent him. I really do."

"Maybe so," Trisha said. "Maybe so."

"He's such a wonderful boy, Strip."

"Yes."

"Very emotional boy. Of course, we don't want to hang onto him or nothing like that. We just want to help him get started. We don't want happening to him what happened . . ." Her voice broke. "Excuse me."

"You don't have to apologize."

"Wait. I hear 'em."

Trisha hurried through the door and was outside just in time to see Strip climbing down from Tom McAlister's pick-up. He had a bag of groceries in his arm. Trisha heard him gasp as he saw her. He froze for a moment. Then, very deliberately, he put the groceries down on the ground, let out a yell, and ran to her.

Trisha was shaking with excitement. She welcomed Strip into her arms and they whirled around, picking each other off the ground.

"It's not you. It can't be you," he said.

"Oh, yes, it is." What she wanted to do was kiss him passionately on the mouth, but she was conscious of the McAlisters. Big Tom looked on from the truck. Margie stood in the doorway of the tiny house.

"So how come you tracked me down here?" Strip said, his voice high with excitement, his eyes round. "Didn't you think I'd be in Vegas?"

"No," she said, a little serious. "I thought you'd be here. And I think you made a good choice."

"So do I. What about you? How you doin'?" He was dying to ask if she was back with Stu.

"I'm doing fine, now. I had to see you."

"I didn't think I should see you."

"You were wrong," Trisha said.

"Good!"

Trisha told Strip to come to her car. She had a couple of things for him. First Strip introduced her to Tom, then the McAlisters went inside.

"You forgot this," Trisha said, handing him the address book.

"I was glad you had it. Trisha. You wore that dress. For me?"

"For you. And here's something else for you."

"What? I forgot something else?"

She handed him a wine bottle wrapped in tissue paper. He unwrapped it nervously and, seeing the message inside, smiled up at her. Their eyes met in perfect complicity, and it was all either could do to keep from embracing. Then neither could not. They kissed each other, lightly, but the touch was precious and intense.

"Go on," Trisha said, making herself stop. "Break it open."

He smashed the bottle on the curb and unfolded the message, reading:

HAPPY BIRTHDAY!

Strip was overcome. He leaned into her and buried his face in her shoulder.

"Wait. Wait, Strip, sweetheart. There's one more thing." She reached in and handed him a gaily wrapped box.

Slowly he unwrapped it. Inside was a Polaroid SX-70 camera.

"Just like yours!"

"It's got more attachments. It's got this thing you can set and run around and take your own picture."

"Show me!"

Trisha explained the timing device and Strip set the camera up on the fender of her car. Then he posed her, triggered the device, and ran to join her.

Together, clasping each other, they watched the image emerge. It was a beautiful shot of them. Together.

The one high school reunion you'll really enjoy!

THE COAST-TO-COAST BESTSELLER

The same high school kids from *Esquire Magazine*'s celebrated "American youth on the verge of a golden era" tell what went right, what went wrong, and...

What Really Happened To
THE CLASS OF '65?

MICHAEL MEDVED AND
DAVID WALLECHINSKY

"Brimming with humor, pathos, mystery, and sex. I couldn't put it down." —HAROLD ROBBINS

With 24 pages of 'Then and Now' photos
Now an NBC-TV series!
𝔅𝔅 A New Ballantine Paperback

NEW FROM BALLANTINE!

FALCONER, John Cheever   27300 $2.25

The unforgettable story of a substantial, middle-class man and the passions that propel him into murder, prison, and an undreamed-of liberation. "CHEEVER'S TRIUMPH . . . A GREAT AMERICAN NOVEL."—*Newsweek*

GOODBYE, W. H. Manville   27118 $2.25

What happens when a woman turns a sexual fantasy into a fatal reality? The erotic thriller of the year! "Powerful."—*Village Voice*. "Hypnotic."—*Cosmopolitan*.

THE CAMERA NEVER BLINKS, Dan Rather
with Mickey Herskowitz   27423 $2.25

In this candid book, the co-editor of "60 Minutes" sketches vivid portraits of numerous personalities including JFK, LBJ and Nixon, and discusses his famous colleagues.

THE DRAGONS OF EDEN, Carl Sagan 26031 $2.25

An exciting and witty exploration of mankind's intelligence from pre-recorded time to the fantasy of a future race, by America's most appealing scientific spokesman.

VALENTINA, Fern Michaels   26011 $1.95

Sold into slavery in the Third Crusade, Valentina becomes a queen, only to find herself a slave to love.

THE BLACK DEATH, Gwyneth Cravens
and John S. Marr   27155 $2.50

A totally plausible novel of the panic that strikes when the bubonic plague devastates New York.

THE FLOWER OF THE STORM,
Beatrice Coogan   27368 $2.50

Love, pride and high drama set against the turbulent background of 19th century Ireland as a beautiful young woman fights for her inheritance and the man she loves.

THE JUDGMENT OF DEKE HUNTER,
George V. Higgins   25862 $1.95

Tough, dirty, shrewd, telling! "The best novel Higgins has written. Deke Hunter should have as many friends as Eddie Coyle."—*Kirkus Reviews*

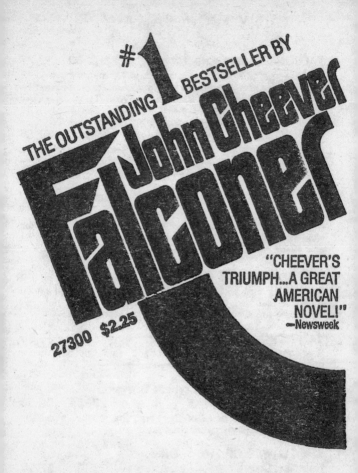